Die for your Friends.

Cal became aware of a harsh humming from behind him. He spun around and found himself facing the grav-sled. Sensor bubbles clung to the underside of the gray slab, like multifaceted fly's eyes.

Cal Shemzak remembered GalFed's orders: "Die before you let the Jaxdron take you. Die for your Friends." Cal looked down at the weapon still gripped in Dr. Ornix's hand. The way Cal Shemzak lived his life demanded only one course of action.

"Hi," he said, raising his arms in surrender and trying to smile through his pain. "Let's be buddies."

The stun beam hit him hard. . . .

Ace Science Fiction Books by David Bischoff

The Star Hounds Series
THE INFINITE BATTLE
GALACTIC WARRIORS (coming in September)

STARHOUNDS

BOOK ONE:
THE INFINITE BATTLE

DAVID BISCHOFF

ACE SCIENCE FICTION BOOKS
NEW YORK

For Henry Morrison

THE INFINITE BATTLE

An Ace Science Fiction Book / published by arrangement with
the author

PRINTING HISTORY
Ace Original / April 1985

ISBN: 0-441-37018-7

Ace Science Fiction Books are published by
The Berkley Publishing Group,
200 Madison Avenue, New York, New York 10016.
PRINTED IN THE UNITED STATES OF AMERICA

Chapter One

HE loved her.

His first thought as he regained consciousness was of her, as though his very ground of being was her.

Laura.

She was there with him, behind his eyes as he struggled up toward waking, her eyes bright, her voice insistent. "Don't die, Cal. Don't die! We are for each other, and I am lost without you."

Opening his eyes, he glimpsed the flash of machinery, the sparkle of glass, the glitter of a starfield through a vu-plate. Then the pain hit him. He shut his eyes and curled into a fetal ball. It was cold, so very cold.

At first he thought he had a hangover. His confused mind searched for the telltale swirl of memory that was the residue of Cal Shemzak on the town. But he drew a blank. Where was the rainbow of drink, the sweet and sour? He had no recollection of women's smiles or the perfume in their hair as he whirled them on the dance floor. No whispery surrender to his virility, either, and he knew despite his closed eyelids that he was alone now.

He was alone and cold, with a head that ached and a stomach that churned with nausea. He fought back the almost overwhelming sensations and opened his eyes.

1

Cal Shemzak lay naked upon a cool length of some silvery alloy. The slab connected to a smooth obsidian wall that seemed to roil with darkness. The floor was riveted metal. One wall was slotted by a view of raw, star-spotted space. Four meters above him, the ceiling hovered like smoked glass.

I'm on a starship, Cal Shemzak thought, shivering. Bile was bitter at the back of his throat, but he controlled his urge to vomit. *A starship . . . but I'm not supposed to be on a starship!*

He looked down at his naked body. A pool of blood lay by a nasty gash in his knee. His hands were scraped raw, and his wakening nostrils were filled with the rancid odor of burnt hair.

"Laura," he said, with sudden conviction. "Laura, I'll never see you—" But no sooner did the thought form than he rejected it. He filled his mind with complex computations and formulas, solving random equations, inventing new ones. He rejected the chill in his body, and suddenly it was not so bad. Woozily he pushed himself up into a sitting position, slowly allowing coherent thought to enter again through his defense shield of mathematics. "Follow the *wo wei*," he told himself in the chant that he and Laura had sung so many times. "Follow the *wo wei*."

The pain dimmed. The room within the mysterious starship sharpened into focus.

Abruptly Cal Shemzak realized where he was.

He was on an *alien* starship.

And with that realization came the memory, which started with the pain of a real hangover.

Cal Shemzak, postadolescent wunderkind, had a hangover.

"I just don't know, Torl," he told his project supervisor, Dr. Torlos Ornix, as they sipped coffee above the whirring engines of the Causal Field Matrix Generator that Cal had helped to design. Neither he nor his thin, dapper companion was aware of the two Jaxdron whipships preparing to crack through the cloudy atmosphere of Mulliphen. Shemzak brushed back a shock of sandy

hair and readjusted his Visual Augmenter implant, an action that drove a spike of pain through his cerebral cortex. He ignored the sensation (Brains don't feel pain!) and scanned the color-depthed holographic readout from the Compunet Analyzer, trying to ascertain a shading of quark action. (Charming, he thought.) "This shows just what all the other charts show, Torl . . . no patterns. Totally random activity on the Prediction Gradients, and numbers that make nonsense of the Reality Window." He looked up pleadingly, his pupils huge owing to the augmenter action. "Let me get a No-Man in here, Torl. I know they're dangerous, but there's no way we can make the Piercing with just this machine!"

"Hot time at the Go-show last night, eh, Cal?" Torl took out a pack of cigarettes, withdrew one, and lit it. Cal Shemzak cringed at the acrid odor of the awful Beta Ophiuchi tobacco that his boss smoked. "Still enjoying the liberties provided by a colony planet? Now, what would Friend Chivon Lasster back on Earth say to a detailed documenting of your debauches?"

"Irrelevant data," Cal said, smiling, as he took out another pill and chased it with a swallow of black coffee. "Or should I say irrelevant date?*"*

"Oh ho, a pretty one you found, then, Cal?" Torl clucked his tongue. "Now what would sister Laura have to say?"

Cal snorted, already feeling a wave of relaxation from the Washpill. The second one always did the trick. Better living through chemistry! "Laura? Laura wouldn't know what a good time was if it walked up and asked the time of day. About the only joy Laura gets out of life is when she gets stuck into one of those blip-ships of hers." Cal shuddered as a wave of regret swept through him. He hadn't seen Laura in months and he missed her badly. "Anyway, Torl, I am serious here." He rattled the stiff holograph chart. "Unless we make some significant changes, we are going to have to report the exact same results to Friend Lasster as last quarter. Namely, absolutely zip!"

The supervisor pursed his lips and tapped ash into a

tray. Smoke wound around his head in translucent threads. "Don't you like it here, Cal?" he asked with a casual, encompassing gesture. "A world light-years from stuffy old Central's nosy snuffling, assigned to a project already listed in the 'improbable' category. Plenty of recreational time on a planet with plenty of distractions, several fascinating alien races, an interesting ecology . . . and a healthy salary."

Cal shook his head. *"I've heard this one too many times, Torl. This place may be Wonder World to you, but frankly I sometimes wonder what the hell I'm doing on it. In case you haven't noticed, I actually care about being a Quantaphys."* He chuckled. *"Even more than having a good time with some hot numbers on the Slippery Track, no matter what you say. This is important stuff, Torl, explosive stuff, and I still can't figure out why the Freaky Feddies put the project so damned close to Jaxdron space."*

"You know this is the closest habitable world to the Fault, Cal," Torl responded coolly.

"Yeah. The Fault. Dr. Hindrix and all that. Well, I'm sorry, and you can attribute it to my recent less than successful graduation from adolescent rebelliousness, but I'm not sure if I buy the company line on physics. A lot of what they taught me doesn't cut the mustard empirically."

Torl smiled sardonically. *"You certainly love your words, don't you, Cal? Take it from an oldster. Enjoy what you've got. Don't look too deeply into everything, it doesn't bear scrutiny. And above all, don't rock the boat, Cal Shemzak! You're not the only person in it, you know."*

"Yeah. I know." Cal got up, unable to hide the slight air of contempt in his voice. *Even though this planet, Mulliphen, was many light-years from GalFedCent, even though it was just a meteor's throw away from a number of Free Worlds, the iron fingers of the Friends hovered at the top of every string of every puppet here.*

Mulliphen was one of the many worlds in the Human Zone considered "Earth standard." The uniqueness of the world was that it lay so close to what Terran physicists had dubbed "the Fault," a disruption of energy flow in Underspace. It was appropriate that the Federation use its beachhead upon this distant world to study the disruption with a team of physicists and engineers. Not that the Friends really gave a hoot in a hand basket about the beauties of physics, Cal Shemzak knew. They just wanted more power.

Cal Shemzak selected his breakfast—eggs, bacon, and toast; his usual—thankful that he didn't have to eat the Shift-stew glop the natives sold to the Earthies. Not that Shift-stew wasn't checked out first for its wholesomeness. Nutritionally it was absolutely top-drawer stuff. The greenish purple color was never particularly appetizing, though, at the best of times. And one never knew exactly what the source of the proteins, carbs, and fat was. The station had all kinds of rumors, to be sure, none savory, but the sweet-natured Mulliphenians merely smiled wistfully when questioned and sang a song or spoke of the weather.

Anyway, Shift-stew was definitely not a post-hangover kind of meal.

Cal Shemzak clopped his plate onto the table beside Dr. Ornix. "Sorry, Torl. Maybe you're right. Besides, what can I do?"

Torl's face seemed to relax at this, which was just what Cal wanted. No good letting the management know your true feelings. He was very close to getting a real tachyonic tailspin from the tonal to the naugul, and the boys in charge would have fits if they ever realized the implications of his work.

"Revolutionary" was the only word that fit, and any form of revolution turned the Friends a little red around the gills. At the best of times the leaders of the Federation government were called benevolent tyrants by their opposition, and though Cal Shemzak somewhat questioned the descriptive noun, he definitely doubted the preceding adjective.

"You are a welcome addition to the team, Cal," Dr. Torlos Ornix said. "I suppose it's understandable that your innovative mind champs at the bit that feeds you."

Cal Shemzak concealed his chuckle at this, concen-

trating on getting his food down.

Breakfast dishes were pushed to one side and the two scientists were absorbed in studying the holocharts when the Jaxdron struck like hammers from the sky.

They first felt it as a vibration deep in the guts of the Matrix Generator.

"What's going on here?" Dr. Torlos Ornix said, staring down at his cup of tea as it clattered in its saucer. Cal Shemzak's coffee mug wobbled off the table and shattered on the floor, splashing the men's shoes with the remains of its contents.

"I don't know!" Cal shouted. His teeth ached from the subauditory rumble; he lost his vision momentarily as the Visual Augmenter ejected its crystalline components onto the table before they could shatter in his eye. This should not happen, Cal Shemzak realized. The vibration buffers on the generator were the most sophisticated in the universe.

"We've got to get down to the engines," Torl was saying as the sound overwhelmed him, rising from a gravelly hum into unbearable volume, then modulating to a siren-like keening. Torl clamped his hands to his ears. His eyes bulged from their sockets. The sound seemed to rip Cal's breath from his lungs. One moment he was sitting, the next he found himself lying on the floor.

"Get out," he yelled as he strained to lift himself up. "We're sitting on a volcano."

A thin stream of blood leaked down Dr. Ornix's left earlobe, dripping into his neat beard. He clung to the table, which was bolted to the floor. The high keen lowered to a steady throb, and Cal became aware of people screaming. He knew that, on the lower levels, people would be scurrying up ladders, climbing stairs, getting out.

Then the explosion came.

It hurled Cal Shemzak off his feet and slammed him into a wall. A girder fell onto the table, smashing it into the floor, barely missing Dr. Ornix, who crawled away beneath the rain of plaster and paper. From below, a kind of obscene gargling sound arose. From the central well shaft connecting the generator's subterranean bulk and the surface operations—solar interaction, atmosphere conditioning, temperature control—a geyser rose like a breath from hell. Fire, shifting curtains of energy, firecracker blossoms of color gathered into a searing maelstrom.

Momentarily stunned, Cal recovered, picked himself up, and ran to Dr. Ornix. "This way," he called. The doctor did not resist as Cal tugged at him. One thing to say about the Fed's projects—they did not stint on safety. Their emergency precautions were as modern and as thorough as possible. Cal guided Dr. Ornix to the nearest blow-pod. "Help me uncycle the door," he cried. Dr. Ornix nodded and together, as the building began to buckle and crack and dissolve around them, they turned the locking wheel. After a moment of resistance it spun. The door opened. Cal pushed his companion into the padded cell, then followed, closing the door behind him.

"Come on, man!" he yelled at the dazed Ornix. "Strap yourself in!" Cal pushed the eject button, then used the ten seconds it took for the pod to activate to buckle into the molded cushion.

Despite the padding, despite the comfortable design of the escape pod, when it rocketed away from the Generator Building the experience was akin to rolling bare-assed down a rocky slope. Dr. Ornix lost consciousness. Cal's world whirled head over heels as the pod lifted into a short trajectory, then headed downward into the Catchfield two hundred meters away.

Unfortunately, the Catchfield was off. When the pod landed, it landed hard, and if not for the cushioning, Cal knew, he and the doctor would have resembled a bowl of Shift-stew moments after impact. When the spherical pod finally rolled to a stop, Cal felt as though his arms and legs had been pulled from their sockets. He seemed a series of aches linked together to form a human being.

Painfully, the taste of blood coppery in his mouth, he unfastened the buckles and pushed away the cushion straps. *"Torl,"* he said. *"Wake up."* He slapped the doctor's face lightly. *"We've got to get out of here!"*

Dr. Torlos Ornix woke into something close enough to consciousness for him to be moved about. Cal removed the doctor's harnesses, then kicked open the escape hatch.

They crawled out onto the grassy field. Other pods had already landed. Generator technicians struggled out, bloody, burned, bruised. Another pod landed hard and rolled into a stand of vlack trees. A group of natives—short humanoids with three sets of hands and long stiff hair covering their bodies—helped the occupants out.

"Oh, my dear God!" came a cry. Cal Shemzak turned to see Shyla Armstile, assistant chief operations director and his occasional girl friend point back to the compound.

The Generator Building was constructed like a mountain: a mountain with levels, a subtle pyramid of levels, much of its operational tubing and piping external rather than internal, but formed in an aethestically pleasing fashion.

Now the building that housed the Casual Field Matrix Generator seemed to shiver as though it had turned to flesh and that flesh were terribly cold. Chunks of the structure had fallen off. Fluid spewed. Electrical lines sparked.

The energy geyser that Cal had observed in the core well was slowly rising from the peak of the mountain-building, reaching for the sky.

And then the whole building simply disappeared.

It phased out of existence, like a dream upon waking.

Moments later there was a loud thunderclap as the surrounding air rushed in to fill the vacuum.

People still dragged themselves from their pods, stunned. The natives danced to and fro, helping them, chittering their squeaking language, pointing back to where the Generator Building had once stood, and to the devastated periphery.

A silence hung over all, an eye-of-the-hurricane silence. Cal Shemzak staggered over to attend to Dr. Ornix, who was leaning now against the battered casing of the pod.

"What could have caused . . . ?" Torl muttered through broken teeth, gazing blankly over Cal's shoulder. "Oh, my God!"

Cal swiveled. At first he saw nothing—and then he saw the ship, descending.

Cal had never seen a Jaxdron ship before. He had seen pictures, and the models used in the war films that had become popular since the start of the First Galactic War five years ago. All had been inaccurate, Cal thought with irony as the real McCoy thundered down on retro-rockets and shimmering repulsor beams. The human renderings of the whip-ships were too symmetrical. The Jaxdron ship that landed a hundred yards away was a jumble of alien geometry, a jagged cluster of angles and rods and nameless shapes.

"The Jaxdrons," Cal said. "They did this. But how?"

"Where are our defense ships?" Dr. Ornix said, suddenly lucid in terror.

Cal shook his head. "Orbital debris, no doubt."

Humans and Mulliphenians were already running away from the imposing shape of the Jaxdron ship.

"Let's get out of here," Ornix said.

"But where to?"

Before they could do anything, however, a triangular-shaped piece of the Jaxdron ship detached itself from the hull and rocketed over the field, knifing through the air.

Cal looked over to Ornix to see if the man had any suggestions. The doctor was staring down, horrified, at the pinkie finger of his left hand.

The finger glowed red for two seconds, then pulsed to blue, then back to red.

"Oh Jesus!" Ornix said. "But it was an approved prosthesis!" He looked up with a stunned expression. "It was from Pax Industries, on Walthor!" Angrily, he tore the hand from his arm. Gray fluid flowed from his stump. The pinkie still pulsed and the digits writhed.

The swift Jaxdron air-sled swooped toward them.

Dr. Ornix looked up at Cal. "It must be you they want," he whispered harshly.

"What are you talking about?" Cal said, suddenly not certain of his grip on reality.

"Things about you that you are not aware of," Ornix said, reaching into a jacket pocket. "Aspects of your work. We were so blind, so stupid not to see!" He pulled out a mini-needler and aimed it at Cal. "I'm sorry, Shemzak, but we can't let them have you."

Cal Shemzak should have died then: the needler beam was directed right at his heart. But Dr. Torlos Ornix froze, eyes glazed over. A wisp of smoke rose from his head. A puff of fire licked up his scalp. He flopped forward, legs twitching, a hole burned through his head.

Cal became aware of a harsh humming from behind him. He spun around and found himself facing the grav-sled. Sensor bubbles clung to the underside of the gray slab, like multifaceted fly's eyes.

Cal Shemzak remembered GalFed's orders. "Die before you let the Jaxdron take you. Die for your Friends." Cal looked down at the weapon still gripped in Dr. Ornix's hand. The way Cal Shemzak lived his life demanded only one course of action.

"Hi," he said, raising his arms in surrender and trying to smile through his headache. "Let's be buddies."

The stun beam hit him hard.

Cal Shemzak groaned as the last of the memory swept through him. He tried to stand, to get off this table, to walk, to do something to get his circulation flowing again, but could not.

He looked up at the ceiling and the clouds seemed to move, as though making way for a clearer view of sky.

A peace settled upon him. He lay back upon the table, no longer cold, but calm, only vaguely aware of pink light spilling down from above him.

The headache was gone. All his pain was gone.

"Laura," he whispered before sleep sent him to an even gentler place.

He loved her.

Chapter Two

IT was the kind of world that might have inspired Dante. An uninformed visitor might see it as a planet of the damned, a world of the doomed. Not that it was barren or hellishly hot, or tundra-cold. On the contrary, its physical properties made it look like some tropical paradise. An eighty-six-degree axial tilt and a regular orbit, combined with a high water-land ratio, made it a planet lush with life, both flora and fauna. Three separate kinds of intelligent alien life—all agricultural/hunters and preindustrial—had developed on the verdant continents. These races were, on the whole, peaceful until Discovery Day. Then the Federation arrived. They saw that this world, listed on the charts as AB 40, second planet of six around the primary Delta Theta, was perfect for the biotechnical ecoforming techniques Federation scientists had perfected. They created an ideal prison world of magnificent utility, far enough from the main thoroughfares of galactic life not to be examined too closely by individuals with a conscience.

The Intelligence operative deep in the corridors of the World's Heart Computer knew this. She also knew that an agent with access to the core data banks within the Block—the castlelike monolith that controlled the planet—could steal priceless information of incredible variety. That was why she had come here, posing as a biotech specialist, and infiltrated the upper-echelon of the Controllers of the Industries. That was why she was padding down the steel corridors as stealthily as a bit of hidden current in a mainframe. The woman had come to open that core, a job deemed totally impossible by the experts.

But the woman was no ordinary intelligence agent.

The guard at the last door was a Conglomerate—a strange fusion of human, alien, and machine manufactured by the ecoindustrial process of this weird world. His antennae wobbled as he reached out to take her pass. Other appendages positioned the identiscreen sensors for retinal readings and additional security checks.

The woman reached across the desk swiftly, and a stunning jolt of electricity at just the right amperage passed from her hand to a control plate in the creature's squat neck, rendering it unconscious. Its oddly jointed limbs twitched as she carefully removed the creature's identity wires. She unbuttoned the loose workblouse she wore, lifted skin flaps, and attached the jacks to her own subcutaneous biotech apparatus.

For all practical purposes, for the next few minutes, until the system destabilized, the security devices would read her as the guard. It had taken a lot of hard work to buy just a short time—and if she wasn't done within the time allowed, laser beams would align on her and burn her body to a cinder.

The agent smiled as she tapped in the opening codes. There was no possible way to finish the job wearing this security identity; she needed more time than it would provide. And when her identity dissolved, and the alarms rang, and all of the multibillion-credit defense weaponry was alerted that an unwelcomed entity was moving about in its most private places . . .

Well, she really wasn't certain what would happen then. No one had ever made it back to tell her.

But one thing was for sure, the agent thought to herself confidently as a static hiss marked the opening of the thick door: when those klaxons blew, and those guns had her in their photonet cross hairs, the drudgery of this assignment would end and the real fun would begin.

Quickly she slipped the guard's needle pistol from its holster and ran through the open door into the unknown.

Immediately she was presented with a choice: three separate corridors confronted her at thirty-degree angles. Tubing and wiring gleamed softly in the corridors' lambent lighting. The smell was, if anything, even more antiseptic than in the rest of the building, the familiar ozonish taste of electricity in the air.

Though she did not know which was the correct way, the agent hardly paused. The rubberized soles of her shoes smacked the tile floor of the rightmost corridor almost instantly.

It took less than thirty seconds to reach a location which, according to her cyborg sensors, was a tapping place. She unscrewed a panel and found the appropriate microchip grid. Less than another forty-five seconds later her biotech consciousness was roving freely through the systems, piercing past the macros of the languages the vast computer understood, skirting even the machine codes, and diving directly into endless kilometers of microchips, understanding their complexities with a power that was beyond analysis, close to intuition.

At her touch the entire security network shut down. The agent chided herself; her estimates had been wrong. She wouldn't have to dodge laser beams after all. Damn, and she had been looking forward to some significant exercise here!

With only a few moments' pause, her mind intuitively found its way through to the top-secret data banks, tapped what they needed, then sped back to the agent's corporeal form.

Dizzily she blinked. Even though she was accustomed to biotech transference, the stepping up of her mind through the macro circuits of the computer, the withdrawal was a heady rush, a sensation of almost druglike intensity. But she had what she needed stored in the microbanks wrapped around her internal organs, and she had made the necessary adjustments inside the computer; no sense sticking around.

Quickly she ran back to the security guard, plugged its identity wires back, retraced her path through the other security measures she had passed to get there, then boarded an elevator.

The Governor of this world lived on the top floor of this massive citadel, in a penthouse restricted to a very few. With her new powers over the controlling computer network, the agent was inside the man's quarters within minutes.

He was sound asleep in his bed, snoring.

The agent walked to his bedside, cocked a forefinger, and placed it against the man's temple.

"Bang," she said. "You're dead."

The man jumped up, startled, but the agent pushed him back, holding him down, fingers nimbly finding pressure points. She laughed.

"Who are you?" the man demanded.

"My name, Governor Bartlick, is Laura Shemzak. I am an operative of the Federation. Your security measures have been tested and found wanting. You will receive a report soon on the necessary methods for strengthening them, after my return to Earth from Walthor."

The man blinked. "But how did you get in here?"

"That will all be in the report, Governor." She released him and stepped back, holding up her empty hands to show that she meant no harm. "Now, may I have a drink? I'm very thirsty."

Still bemused, the man put on a dressing gown. The agent—Laura Shemzak—followed him into his office, where she sat quite arrogantly behind the man's desk and accepted a bottled soda. She also used a few names and phrases that established the validity of her claimed identity. Governor Bartlick was then eager to please this astonishing visitor.

"I must admit," the gray-haired man said, pouring

himself a drink more alcoholic than soda, "that I am astonished. I personally selected the security chief. I hope you will stay long enough to go over this affair in some detail, so that we can take measures against this happening again. What with the Jaxdron war and everything, the Federation simply cannot afford to have a vulnerable security system here at Pax Industries. Especially given the sort of thing that happened on Mulliphen."

Laura sat up. "Mulliphen? What happened on Mulliphen?"

"Oh yes, you would not have heard. Terrible business. Jaxdron attack. Just received a communiqué on FedNews this evening."

Laura stood. "Jaxdron attack?"

"Yes, I suppose that would interest you," the Governor said. "The news release is somewhere in that pile of papers."

It did not take long for Laura to find the report that Governor Bartlick referred to.

She read it quickly, and then she read it again.

She took a long breath.

"When's the next flight out of here?" the agent demanded.

"Can't you stay?" the man asked. "I really would like you to speak to the security chief personally."

"That's impossible," she said curtly. Then her voice softened. "According to this, Governor, the Jaxdron kidnapped one of the scientists working on the project on Mulliphen, someone of extreme importance to me."

"But you can't just break into my computer system and then leave!" the Governor said.

"Can't I?" the agent said. "Governor, I'll work up a full report in transit to Earth. In the meantime, just watch my smoke!"

Chapter Three

"LAURA Shemzak," the woman said. "I am Friend Chivon Lasster."

"It's about goddamned time!" Laura said.

"I am a busy officer, Laura." The woman stared placidly from behind her desk, her expression and voice cool. "You are fortunate to find yourself an audience with a Friend so soon."

Laura slammed her hand on the desk. "Cut the crap, stoneface. I'm getting to talk to you because I'm hot stuff in your damned Intelligence Net, and you bloody well know it." She leaned over the desk, and if her reach had been longer, or the desk less wide, she would have grabbed the officious bitch by her wide black lapels and shaken her hard. "Now, where the hell is my brother? Tell me what has happened to Cal Shemzak!"

An eyebrow raised into the blond bangs of Friend Lasster's pageboy haircut. "Was the Intelligence brief insufficient? There was a Jaxdron raid on Mulliphen last week. Cal Shemzak was captured. There are oddments of other facts, mostly irrelevant. But the central fact is that there is simply nothing we can do. The Jaxdron have the man you call your 'brother.'" A faint sneer came to Friend Lasster's lips at the archaic term. "And unless they choose to return him, with heartfelt apologies no doubt, you are not likely to see him again.''

Laura Shemzak stared eye to eye with the older woman, as though that alone could work her will. After a moment of steely silence she spoke, tersely. "You fit me with a blip-ship, and I'll find him.''

The woman behind the desk leaned back in her chair and laughed derisively. She turned and thumbed a control. A holocomp display activated. Pressing appropriate buttons conjured a series of readouts—ghost letters hanging in the air. Friend Lasster's eyes brushed over these casually, then fixed upon Laura Shemzak.

"Ah yes,'' she said. "I forgot about your specialty. You appear to be quite a unique operative.'' Her tone of voice changed to calm respect. "You are to be commended.''

"I *have* been, thank you.'' Laura said, dark eyes blazing. "And now I want cooperation!'' Her face, when less constricted with fury, might be called beautiful, with its perfectly tapered nose, high cheekbones, thick black eyebrows. Now, though, severity masked any loveliness. High glossy boots added a good eight centimeters to her short stature. She wore a black jump suit, black turtleneck, and black gloves: her usual attire. Her black hair was clipped short. The only color to her was the cream of her face, the specks of green in her eyes, and a blood-red scarf tied casually around her neck. "I've been serving you frakking bureaucrats for four years now, doing your dirty-laundry Intelligence work and testing your new equipment on the side. You bastards owe me, and I intend to collect.''

"I take it that what you mean to collect is one blip-ship, to hop in and streak off into an area of trillions of square kilometers of unknown space in search of one lowly individual. You lend the phrase 'needle in a haystack' new meaning, Laura Shemzak.''

"Get your head out of the clouds, lady,'' Laura said, stalking around the side of the desk and pushing a code into the keyboard of the holocomp. "You think I'm stupid? I work for IntelNet, remember. I've got access to just as much of the inside scoop as you do."

Colors danced. Figures swirled in the air like a bunch of silent but angry insects, eventually collecting into an uneasy hover. Laura stabbed her fingers through the holograph. "Can you read this, Lasster?"

Friend Lasster could not hide her annoyance. "With my Interpret Compiler, yes."

"Well, I can read the raw stuff, Lasster. There was just enough machinery operating in the wreckage of Mulliphen's defense systems to put a tracer on those Jaxdron whip-ships. They're headed in a direction that could only take them one place . . . Baleful. Coridian system, Marchgild sector. The first territory the bastards grabbed when they made their move five years ago. You remember Baleful, don't you? Right by those binaries: the Witch's Tits. Smack dab in the center of the Underspace Fault, too, which is probably why they kidnapped Cal. Baleful used to be ours, remember? We've got memory bytes up the wazoo on Baleful, to say nothing of projections and simulations. . . . Hell, the only problem with you Friends is that you ain't got the frakking *cojones* to even ponder some kind of rescue mission. You ought to thank me for taking it upon my able shoulders to deal with this crisis situation."

She grinned, showing teeth faintly stained by *rictori* smoke.

"And you volunteer for this—ah—duty purely out of the kindness of your heart, to say nothing of the vast respect you have for the Friends and our government." Lasster's voice was sharp with sarcasm.

Laura folded her arms against her chest and kept her grin. "Yeah."

Friend Chivon Lasster swiveled and went to her bar for a drink. "Only very special Friends are permitted alcoholic beverages in their offices." She plopped ice into a glass, added a spill of sparkle whiskey. "My weakness, Laura. Would you care for some?"

"Uh uh. Slaughters my serotonin."

Lasster drank. "Now, your motivation for this gallant gallivanting is not precisely as clear as you declare, is it? You see, I, too, have access to certain memory areas . . . areas that even you cannot delve into."

"Maybe I don't want to. Maybe I'm too much a lady to muck about in that junk," said Laura, unable to conceal her defensiveness.

"I took the time this morning, Laura Shemzak, to avail myself of my unladylike abilities." Lasster sipped at the cool, effervescent drink and stared into a shifting mood sculpture. The lights, previously playful, darkened into shadowplay. "An interesting little story, Laura, one which, as a Friend responsible for the stability of the state's homeostasis, I can hardly condone."

"No one asked you, you frakking bitch," Laura Shemzak shot back.

"Sticks and stones, blippie."

Laura cringed at the word. She turned away to hide any vulnerability that might wash over her face.

"It makes for an interesting aberration, Shemzak. A tale of . . . what is the archaic term? . . . ah yes, sentimentality worthy of some squalid colony. A male and female from the same brood vats accidentally placed in the same growschool, developing an attachment, and then, coincidence piled upon accident, discovering their fleshly relationship."

"Brother . . ." said Laura. "And sister. Can't you say it, Friend Lasster? Just pairings of syllables like any other words."

". . . . flesh pairs, as I said, who found some perverted thrill in that knowledge, and in the concealment of that knowledge from Friends, from the authoritative system that created you," Chivon Lasster continued stiffly. "And in your perversity you created a rebellious bond, a bond whose value you clearly place far above your duties and fealty sworn to your creators."

Laura shrugged. "We've done a damned fine job for you, all of you. Our relationship . . . our love"—she spat the word out spitefully—"for each other has never interfered with performance of what our Aptitude Training Vectors have led us to. Look, Friend Lasster," she said in a softer voice, "all I ask is for the chance to find Cal, a chance that only someone with my abilities might have.''

"All we can do now, Laura Shemzak, is to take your request under consideration. Your work has been good and—''

"Consideration?" Laura almost yelled. "Time is at a premium here! I must do this now. Who knows—''

A chime sounded, interrupting Laura's frustrated harangue. They both turned to see a door behind Chivon Lasster's desk sliding open. This was not the door she had used to come in, Laura realized.

A man entered the room, wearing a military outfit. His features were sharp, his eyes canny. "Pardon my intrusion, Friend Lasster. But you did say that Citizen Laura Shemzak was due for an audience at this time. And I can see that though I am not prompt, Laura Shemzak is. Good day to you, Laura."

Perplexed, Laura nodded.

"I do believe I can handle this matter, Friend Zarpfrin," Lasster said testily.

"You forget, Friend Lasster, that as soon as any matter pertaining to the Jaxdrons leaves human-inhabited space, it enters my domain." The officer had a high, shiny forehead and a prissy demeanor enhanced by the height at which he held his round nose.

"How did you learn of this matter?"

Laura saw the annoyance in Chivon Lasster's attitude and struck while the iron was hot. "I'm sure that Friend Zarpfrin can read as well as you or I. Now, what I propose, Zarpfrin, is this: you provide me with a blip-ship and I'll do the rest."

"If Zarpfrin can read, he can also hear, and I'm sure he's been listening to our conversation and knows of your request."

Zarpfrin parted with a reassuring smile. "Through the privacy filter, Friend Lasster, as required. Now, as to Cal Shemzak, though . . . we naturally regret his loss, Laura, but he is expendable. Besides, a venture into Jaxdron-held space, even for a woman with your . . . odd and unique abilities, even with the use of a blip-ship

. . . why, that would be tantamount to suicide."

Laura smiled. "Yeah."

"Then what you are suggesting is that we sacrifice one of our top agents, to say nothing of an expensive starship, for the slim chance of retrieving a man we don't really need?"

"I have a considerable bank account, as your files will no doubt tell you, Lasster," said Laura. "How about if I put that up as a deposit against any blip-ship loaned to me?"

"Ludicrous," said Lasster.

The other Friend held up a hand. "Now now, Friend Lasster, I have been taking this matter under heavy consideration and have even discussed it with the Council of Five—"

"The Five . . . You went above my—"

"Time is of the utmost value here, as I am sure we are all aware. Now, as we have indicated, the Mulliphen incident has already been very costly to us, and the loss of Cal Shemzak is something we were prepared to write off. However, Citizen Shemzak's brave request alters matters considerably." He turned limpid eyes back to Laura, and for the first time ever in her dealings with the Friends she saw a speck of kindness. "We would certainly like to see Cal Shemzak returned to his state duties, even though, as you know, we are required to strongly disapprove of the relationship you claim. However, we would also very much like to have a look at Jaxdron operations on Baleful, as that beachhead is one of several which may be involved with military maneuvers to come."

"Why can't you just speak plainly, man?" Laura said, excited but also annoyed. "You want me to scout weapons placement. And unless I miss my guess, if I can manage to do that, it doesn't make a hell of a lot of difference whether I return or not, as long as I subspace-radio the details."

Lasster's face resumed its marblelike coolness. "Still a foolhardy mission."

"A human with a mission is not a fool, Friend

Lasster." He turned back to Laura Shemzak. "Though your reasons oppose Friendhood standards, the council finds no reason why we should not use them to our advantage. Knowing this, do you still want to undertake this journey?"

"You bet your balls I do!" Laura grinned over with triumph at Lasster, who swallowed the last of her drink and poured some more. "Just give me a ship and I'm ready to trip!"

"It's a little more complicated than that, I'm afraid," said Friend Zarpfrin. "Naturally, for the sake of the mission's success, we wish you to utilize the latest-model blip-ship—"

"Hot damn. . . . Not the Armageddon Special!"

"The XT Mark Nine, to be exact."

"Well, they're still testing those at the factory on Shortchild in the Capellan system, I thought."

"Yes. We can immediately arrange for your transport to Shortchild, and will naturally subspace instructions to the office on that planet. When you arrive, the Mark Nine should be ready for your use. Fortunately, Capella is on the way toward Jaxdron space anyway."

"Now, that's what I call serendipity! I'm set to go."

"One little detail, but an important detail, Laura," Friend Zarpfrin said. "The Mark Nine is a signficant advance over the other vessels in the XT line. Proper use of its full capacity requires an adjustment in your cyborg systems."

"Okay, so you're going to poke around in me some more. That doesn't take long. It's not like you've never put the screws to me before."

"Excellent. You shall be escorted to the nearest biomech hosp, where you will meet our specialist, Dr. Minz."

"What happened to Hamsin? He's my usual med," Laura said, for the first time feeling some small concern. She had grown to trust Dr. Hamsin. He'd been with her from the very beginning of the mech operations, when she was just eleven years old.

"Dr. Minz has been specially trained to deal with the

bio-applications of the new parameters of the XT series, Citizen Shemzak. This will only require the afternoon and the evening. Following a short sleep, you will be dispatched to the next transport to Shortchild."

"Thank you, Friend Zarpfrin, and please thank the council as well." She shot a hateful glance toward Chivon Lasster. "It was clear that I was barking up the wrong tree in this office."

"Friend Lasster," said Friend Zarpfrin, "would you kindly arrange for Citizen Shemzak's transportation to biomech facilities? And then I should like to have a brief meeting with you, concerning your attitude in this matter."

Laura Shemzak shot Chivon Lasster a victorious look. *Don't worry, Cal,* she thought. *Your sister's coming to get you!*

Chapter Four

WHEN Cal Shemzak woke again, he no longer felt any pain. He awoke relaxed and refreshed. "*I feel marvelous,*" he thought, *considering I'm a prisoner on an alien spacecraft.*"

Not only did he feel good; he was also no longer cold. He sat up, noticing that he wore a form-fitting robe, a solid gray in color. Slippers of an identical material—fibrous, silky, but thickly tough—clung to his feet.

He hopped off his slab and looked up at the clouded ceiling. "Hey! Thanks, guys. I feel much better. Are we going to talk now?"

The clouds shifted darkly in response, a tremble of light shuddering through the shadow.

"The strong, silent types, right?" He lifted his robe to check his burned and bruised legs, wondering why he no longer felt pain. His ankles, calves, knees, and thighs, once blackened or bloody, were now unmarked. They were also hairless.

"Holy shit," Cal said, a hand rising instinctively to the top of his scalp.

Baby-rump bald!

"Well, you guys have certainly been busy, haven't you?" Cal said, annoyed despite his renewed sense of well-being. "So, are you going to have the decency to come out and play?"

Silence.

Violet light spasmed through layers of creamy translucence that seemed to stretch upward for many meters.

"Okay. The name is Calispar Shemzak, predoc, University of Alpha Ceti." He grinned. "Correspondence school, mind you. Born under supervised conditions on Terra, serial number A59 Omega Omega Zero 45 Subdivision 12. I want you to know that's all you're going to get from Cal Shemzak!"

Unless, of course, Cal thought, *you threaten to torture me.*

His words reverberated through the chamber, dying off into whispery echoes.

A sudden shaft of bluish light hit the floor two meters from his feet. The base widened, creating a cone of light. Two people—or rather, holograms of people—appeared within the cone, auraed with a ghostly glow.

Cal recognized his sister Laura immediately. It took him a little longer to recognize himself.

The figures were younger versions . . . perhaps fifteen years old. . . .

Four years ago!

". . . . Do you think they know?" Laura was asking. She wore the red-and-white skip suit of a cadet, complete with epaulets and trim.

"No," said Cal's younger image, slouched nonchalantly upon a couch. "But if we keep our promise to each other, they will soon enough. I dare say, knowing these jokers and the kind of important positions we're being trained for, they're going to be screening our mail." He lit his pipe, one of a stream of affectations he used to demonstrate his impending adulthood.

"A code!" Excitement lit her dark eyes, and the older Cal fell in love with her all over again. She looked so much better in long hair. *Wait a minute,* he thought. *How did the Jaxdron get a recording of this conversation?* "We can devise a secret code," Holo-Laura was saying, "consisting of banal everyday words, so they won't even know it's a code. Won't that be fun?"

"Hold on a second, motor mouth," Cal said affectionately. "It's not like we're going to be doing anything wrong. Just unconventional. Society these days looks upon our sort of relationship like . . . well, like farting and belching and picking your nose in public . . . you know, uncivilized, barbaric.''

"But it's not, Cal. It's wonderful.'' She was all smiles then, an innocent little girl, and Cal hated the Friend-hood for what they had done to her in these past four years.

"Yeah, well, just don't wipe your snot on me, okay?'' Cal said, grinning his best mischievous grin.

"Oh, you're awful!'' she said, hitting him playfully. Her blows had been harmless then, but she certainly could pack a wallop these days! These days he watched his mouth around her. "You're the one who found all those delightful old films, those old books.''

"Yeah, and I'm also the one who peeped into those record spools and found out certain relevant genetic in-formation.'' He put his arm around her and hugged her. "We have had a good time, haven't we?''

"We've been naughty!'' she said, her eyes shining as she kissed him on his cheek.

"But we're going to see each other again, whenever possible. And the only way we're going to be able to stay in touch is through letters, so I guess we're just going to have to be a little more obvious about our feel-ings. There will be a lot of frowns, sure, and if our com-panions in our respective schools find out, which they most likely will, we will no doubt get oodles of flak.'' The holo-image of his younger self stood up. "Now then, all packed?''

"Yes.''

"Just remember this, Laura Shemzak. I love you, and I shall always love you. I'm learning in my classes that time and space can just be an illusion, if you want them to be. Let the Friendhood and all its bureaucratic cubbyholes keep its illusions that just because you're go-ing off to be a starship pilot and I'm staying here to jug-gle numbers and symbols, we're going to be apart where it counts. . . .''

Holo-Laura went to hug holo-Cal, and the real Cal Shemzak had to turn away from the interplay of colored light because a pang was forming in his throat and his eyes smarted with tears.

"What are you doing to me, you assholes?" he screamed up at the ceiling clouds. But Cal Shemzak knew full well what they were doing, and he did not like it at all. The Jaxdron were somehow futzing about in his brainbox, tapping into his memories.

"Get out of my head," he yelled, offended to the core of his being at the invasion. "You bastards hear me? Get out of my head!"

He couldn't feel it, but they were somehow dissecting his mind. The Jaxdron paid no attention to Cal's loud complaints, so eventually he just shut up.

Cal and Laura Shemzak might have been whelped from the same womb, he would always tease her, but you could have fooled me! They had different approaches to life. Laura fought things tooth and nail, whereas Cal simply cruised blithely through things. If you're getting raped, he would tell her, you might as well lie back and enjoy it. Laura hated that particular tease, and Cal secretly felt sorry for anyone who tried to rape his sister.

He pulled himself up onto his slab, folded his arms over his chest, and watched the show.

He knew it all, of course, but some of it he had forgotten in recent years; so the significant scenes that began to play across the chamber floor like a ten-ring circus were interesting, the course of his life in bright images and soft sounds.

He chuckled as he watched a particularly cherished memory: the time he had flummoxed the Dayfriends at country school with tales of what the Nightfriends would gossip about them. Cal had always been a playful character, and his jokes were more often practical than verbal. If the heart of Earth society had been the nuclear family, he might have had problems. But since the individuals who cared for the broodgroups did so in shifts, it was child's play to raise hell, and Cal Shemzak, with his sister's help, did just that.

Summerhome; tripschool; winterspill: the scenes from this variety of government raiseplaces continued for some time, forming a fascinating mosaic.

"Trying to figure it all out, huh?" Cal said, addressing the ceiling. "Well, good luck."

Then a particular scene caught his attention, a moment in his past that he did not particularly care to remember; yet he could not turn away.

A boy of seven—himself—was sitting beside a pretty young woman. Her image made Cal's heart leap. It was his favorite Dayfriend, Mirg Lifta.

"Now, Cal," the woman was saying, "you know that this is the way it has to be."

"But why?" The little boy's voice was close to a sob. "I don't want you to leave. You all leave!"

"Now, don't cry. You're much too old to cry. If you can't control that emotionsphere, Cal, I'm going to have to report it to the Overfriends, and they'll give you medication again."

"No," the little boy said. "I'm not crying!" His voice was angry.

"Good. Anger is power, but remember, power needs control. Now, as to my departure: why does it trouble you so, Cal? You know it's part of the rules, and the Overfriends made the rules for the good of their children and for the good of the state. So if we obey those rules, then that makes my leaving good, makes us all good. Don't you want to be good, Cal?"

"No."

"It's not good to be attached. The only true commitment anyone has is to the Microstate of Earth and the Macrostate of the Human Federation."

"Can't you stay just a few more months? I like the games you teach me."

"Well, you're very good at math, Cal, good at these sorts of games. I've recommended you for advanced computer interface, did you know that?"

"No!" the little boy said, unable to hide his excitement. "Thank you."

"And I must go because I must go. This is my job, Cal. I do it not out of any feeling for you children, but because it is my obligation to you as part of this Microstate." The words were soft and considerate . . .

touched with the very feeling they denied. Cal saw a
gleam of wetness in the Dayfriend's eye for just a moment, and then she was under control again.

"I think the state can go to hell and toast to pure carbon!" Cal said viciously.

"Cal, that's treason talk, and we've spoken about
treason talk before. I won't report it. We've had a good
time together, and I don't wish to see it end on a sour
note."

"I'm sorry," the little boy murmured.

"Of course you are. Now, I am already late."

"I'll never see you again."

"There's no rule against seeing each other again, Cal.
But I will be placed on different planets, so it is un-
likely."

The little boy could not look at the pretty Dayfriend
as she rose to leave. Cal could see the struggle to fight
back tears in the little boy's face, and suddenly he
vividly remembered that moment in his past as though it
were happening again.

As the hologram faded away, he found tears leak-
ing down his face, tears that had been stored away, fer-
menting a long time. "Good-bye, Friend Mirg," he
whispered.

All at once he was angry again. He jumped off the
slab and shook his fist upward. "Okay, you wretches.
Alien scumbags! You made me cry. Does that make you
happy? You want a drop of the stuff for your specimen
box? All it is is salinated H_2O, you jerk-off turkeys!"

There was no response to his ranting, and so his rage
spent itself. Realizing he was strangely tired again, Cal
crumpled down to a sitting position on the floor.

"No more show, huh? Got all the info stored away in
the psyche files, right? Good. You know, I'm kind of
hungry. Does this boat have dinner service?"

Again no answer.

"How about a good book? I'm getting pretty damned
bored. In fact, I . . ."

The clouds solidified, opaqued. The ceiling was just a
ceiling again.

With a whir, an outline of a door appeared in the far

wall. The door began to slide open.

Cal jumped up. He wanted to run. But he controlled the emotion and stood his ground.

When the door fully opened, only darkness lay beyond. Then a figure separated itself from the darkness.

"Oh, my God," said Cal Shemzak.

Chapter Five

THE building in Upper Pan-America was a plain, functional sort: blocks on blocks; adhered stone, metal, glass. However, if its sprawling mass was architecturally plain to the casual Denver stroller or motorist, its interior was undeniably remarkable, not merely in context but in content. The plainness concealed the most advanced security system of the human universe: a complex gridwork not merely of alloys and rock but of force fields and energy bafflers. Guarded by a crack military division specifically bred and trained for the task, the Big Box, as it had been dubbed, was also paid special attention by the space weaponry array that guarded the home of humanity in this its most hazardous period in a long and spectacularly troubled history. This was the kernel of Federation government; it was here that the Overfriends—snidely called "the Best Buddies" by the Free Worlds they did not control—kept their offices.

Overfriend Chivon Lasster was, at thirty-three standard Earth years, the fourth youngest member of the august body that guided the course of the Second Galactic Empire. Overfriends were the only group not specifically developed for their particular positions by the sociocultural machinery. Rather, they were the cream of their fields, elected by the other Overfriends after careful screening by the Auditions Council, part of the large network of subofficers called the Underfriends.

Chivon Lasster took great pride and satisfaction in her position. In this neo-Platonic determinist form of government that held the Federated Empire together, the position of Overfriend was the only career one could choose to strive for. Every other social and occupational niche was either genetically or behavioristically preprogrammed. There were plenty of levels of accomplishment within every Calling; achievement and drive were the stuff that fed the energy and motivational drive of the Macrostate. Still, becoming an Overfriend was a rare distinction for an individual, and Chivon privately reveled in her victory—particularly since it gave her the leverage she needed if she was ever to find Tars Northern.

"Sometimes," she told Overfriend Zarpfrin after Laura Shemzak had left, "I wonder if we are not too arch, too tricky for our own good."

"Pardon?" said Zarpfrin, looking up from a study of documents called up from the central computer.

"I mean, there really was no good reason for me to put up any opposition to the woman's volunteering. After all, she's perfect for the mission, and she's come forward exactly at the time we need her. She's playing right into our hands."

"Precisely," said the meticulously groomed man. "Didn't you read the psychoprofile? If we were too cooperative, she's the sort who would be suspicious. Let us just say that all we have done today is to provide an illusory barrier for Laura Shemzak to break through."

"Psychoprofile . . . I only glanced at it, I'm afraid," said Friend Lasster. "Just gleaned something of her background, and that she's a remarkable blip-ship pilot. Which quite surprises me, considering her generally unrefined qualities, her reckless air—she must hide a great deal in ordinary person-to-person dealings. In fact, Overfriend, she seems to me to be far too impetuous, too impulsive to be a logical choice for a Calling of such importance in our military.''

Zarpfrin shook his head. "You should take a moment to study that profile . . . as well as the girl's record. Not only is it fascinating, it's also highly entertaining. Suffice it to say that Laura has mental capacities far enough away from the norm to border on the psychic. Add to those the impetuous and impulsive—and decisive!—nature you have taken note of, and you have a powerful agent in unpredictable situations, where action is necessary immediately.''

"You mean she hardly even thinks about what she's doing?''

"Not consciously, certainly. Her decisions are incredibly quick. Add a mind able to grasp all she needs for piloting our experimental XT's on a subconscious level, and you have a top agent in the field.''

"I don't know, Zarpfrin. She seems awfully slow to pick up on some things—cocky, maybe, but often just stupid.''

"You forget how young she is, Friend Lasster. Her success in the field is not built on hard-gained wisdom, nor on a great deal of knowledge, but on the qualities I have previously described, plus a large measure of self-confidence. As to her coarse nature: that was picked up to survive among the ruffians in the Space Force. She's changed since she was selected for blip-ship training—different posture, accent, world view. What remains is her devotion to her brother—which we are using to our benefit, as you can see.''

"Still, it's hard to imagine her as one of our top Intelligence agents!''

Zarpfrin smiled with genuine amusement. "Let's just say that on the occasions when her hunches are wrong, the results are monumentally catastrophic. But she is rarely totally wrong, though I must say she's landed in some ungodly situations! The entertaining aspect of her profile I spoke of—''

"The mission is as near-impossible as the readout indicates?''

"Deadly,'' said Zarpfrin, standing and smoothing his

costume. "Even with her abilities and the features of the XT Mark Nine, she has about an icicle's chance in Hades of reaching Cal Shemzak in Jaxdron space."

"And if she does?"

"If she does, she has been prepared for that eventuality." Zarpfrin grinned. "In more ways than one."

Chivon nodded.

"I trust you realize, Friend Lasster, that you have been chosen to monitor her mission. I also am paying special attention, which means I may be making trips to the Fringe Worlds. I trust you can handle matters here in that eventuality."

"I think I am one of the few Earth-based Overfriends who actually enjoy interstellar travel," Lasster said, "yet I rarely get the chance these days."

"I've done my share, and I have rather come to loathe it," said Zarpfrin. "Especially in the past five years, with added war duties . . . to say nothing of my little hobby."

"Northern. The council has specifically censured your search, hasn't it?"

A troubled expression flitted over Zarpfrin's firmly set features. Then he smiled grimly. "Call me Ahab."

Chivon Lasster found a shiver passing through her. She poured herself another drink. "I think I have given up," she whispered harshly. "We have that bond, though. This is why we work together so well, I think. This is why I can keep your activities in that area . . . secret."

"An entirely separate matter, dear lady, from the one at hand. One that does not bear mention, actually. You must pardon me, but I must make arrangements for Laura Shemzak's . . . reception . . . at her destination. There are definite prerequisites for the proper function of the XT." Zarpfrin's eyes turned thoughtful. "I do hope she gets back. She does have a certain sexual vitality that strikes my fancy. An imposing potential conquest, I think."

"Your taste in women has been running toward the youngish side lately, Friend Zarpfrin," said Chivon

Lasster distractedly. The liquor wasn't working. She wondered if she should try a pill. She didn't want to call up Andrew today . . . he was getting to be an addiction she didn't care to have.

Zarpfrin smiled gently. "As I pride myself upon my eclectic taste, I take offense at that remark. To paraphrase an old and neglected poet, if variety is the spice of life, season on! Good day, Friend Lasster. I commend you again for your performance."

"I have learned at the feet of a true master."

Overfriend Zarpfrin left, humming a popular tune. Zarpfrin had always been by nature a convivial, if Machiavellian, sort. If not for Tars Northern and the days of the project, he might actually be happy now. He certainly seemed to relish the intrigue and conflict of the Jaxdron war. But if Tars Northern was the emptiness and bitterness in Chivon Lasster's life, then he was the thorn in Zarpfrin's side, and Zarpfrin hated thorns.

Lasster sighed and put down her drink, unfinished. She went back to her desk and attempted some paper work to get her mind off this unsavory matter. Solo work was always a comfort to the efficient woman; she could lose herself, and any troubles, in juggling rows of detail.

After a few minutes, though, it was apparent that she was not running at optimum efficiency. There was something bothering her about all this, some niggling worm of a thought she might call intuition if not for her rigid upbringing. There were troubled emotions deep down as well.

The official position of the Macrostate upon emotions in its constituency was simple. The full spectrum of human feelings was acknowledged; however, only certain types were considered healthful for the greater good. Anger, pride, ambition, hatred, altruism, loyalty: these could be expressed, but emotions not considered fruitful for society were frowned upon. Therefore private disciplines, medications, and more complex methods were used to eradicate these unsocial, painful conditions.

The wealthier members of any Microstate could afford individual psychcomp service. Chivon Lasster did not like to avail herself of her Computer Companion during working hours, but since her productivity was presently curtailed, use of the CompComp was in order.

She connected the necessary ROM chip array to the console, which then gave her access to the megabyte system that belonged to her alone, deep in the CPU of the titanic subterranean computer.

She tapped out her code. Lights paraded across the console. A fountain of color spewed up, taking holographic form.

A man.

She kept sensory toned down. Keep this intellectual, she thought, as the man opened his eyes and looked at her.

"Hello, Andrew," she said to the simulacrum. "I need to talk."

He was dressed in a neat suit. He was quite handsome in an older, fatherly fashion, with white fleecing the sides of his long, styled hair. His blue eyes shone with compassion.

"Times have been hard," he said. "The war is worrisome, and your position here burdens you. And yet I sense that this is not why you need soothing. Pardon my directness, Friend Chivon Lasster, but as your personally designed CompComp, I know you well, and it is my deduction from present sensory input that it is something else that troubles you, something that even we have not spoken of for a while." He paused and sat down on the console, a ghost on a machine. "It is Tars Northern that still troubles you, despite your medication, despite your mental control exercises."

"Yes," said Chivon Lasster, admitting it to the CompComp finally as she buried her face in her hands. "Yes, God help me, that's true."

Chapter Six

THE starship captain brooded over the readings suspended in the small vu-tank. "What do you think, Jitt?" he asked the man sitting in the nearest jockey chair.

"Captain Northern, most respectfully, after much study of the freighter with the help of our highly developed sensor system, I submit that an attempted pirate action would simply be much too dangerous to even contemplate, though we have detected trace amounts of attilium and needed supplies." Fear quivered on the small man's dark face.

Tars Northern chuckled deep in his throat. "Tell me true, Yellowspine, is this based on actual computations of comparative firepower? Or is this simply one of your lily-livered premonitions, derived to keep your own ass high and dry?"

"Truly, Captain," said Dansen Jitt. "Firepower is no problem. A surprise attack would give us the needed edge. Yet I cannot help but think: What if there is a sensor baffler within the freighter, concealing extra Federation forces, skulking in wait for us? What if this is a trap? What if they have new, powerful weapons that will fry us all and the *Starbow* into crispy cinders? What if—"

37

"What if the King of Fomalhaut Three had ovaries!" said a tall blond Amazon of a woman at the doorway to the control cabin. "He'd be Queen!"

"No," said Jitt, his eyebrows knitting with increasing worry. "He'd be a hermaphrodite, which is not uncommon in these days of advanced genetic engineering."

Kat Mizel shook her head and walked up to the captain, handing him a drink. "Thought you might need a relaxant, Tars," she said, with a tender sparkle in her eyes.

"If I wanted one, Kat, I would have asked for one," said Captain Northern in an annoyed tone. He set the drink in a holder without tasting it, turning a granite face away from her. When Tars Northern smiled, he was startlingly handsome, with the kind of eyes, the sort of contemptuously sensuous mouth that women dreamed about. But when he frowned, as he did then, he was ice.

"Look, Tars," said the woman, "just because of one argument you're acting like a little child? Darling, I'm saying I'm sorry. How about a little warmth?" She slipped her hand around his neck, onto his opposite shoulder, sexily toying with an epaulet of his casual uniform.

Northern reached back and plucked her hand away, then spun and fixed her with a steely glance. "Mizel, this is not the time or the place. We are about to begin an important operation, goddammit. Have you no sense of priorities?"

Angrily she flung her long blond hair back, and struck a defiant position, a lithe hip thrust forward, head bent down over large breasts, matching him glare for glare with her violet eyes. "I'm going with the boarding party, then, Tars."

Captain Northern shrugged eloquently. "I'm delighted. Do us all a favor and get shot, okay?" He picked the drink out of the holder and casually flipped it back at her. Instinctively she caught the cup, but its contents spilled out onto her grab-boots. Kat Mizel shrieked, bounced the cup off the floor, then stalked away, cursing. A servo-robot buzzed forward to clean up the mess.

Dansen Jitt poked his head warily from the shelter of his arms, peeking first to make sure the woman was gone. "A very demanding young lady," he said.

"Yeah," said Tars Northern, with a broad smile. "Maybe *that* was the severe danger you saw in the cards, Jitt." Northern played with controls. "Now then. According to the scanner, the Federation Freighter *Ezekiel* will emerge from Underspace beyond the ecliptic plane of this star system in precisely one hour and thirty-two minutes. Dr. Mish is very eager to obtain that attilium, you know, Jitt. We wouldn't want to disappoint him, would we?"

Dansen Jitt sighed. "I don't know why you ask me for my psychic opinion, Captain. You always pooh-pooh it. You just don't appreciate my abilities."

"When a watchman always cries wolf, Dansen Jitt, the wise man waits for the cry 'Wolf pack!' "

"You really don't care about the attilium, do you? You just want the supplies and the money."

Northern shrugged and continued perusing the read-outs.

"And the thrill of tweaking the Federation's nose by using this godforsaken starship. God, this thing does give the creeps sometimes, Captain. I can't sleep nights for the nightmares. It's just not made for humans, I tell you. I don't think—"

"You know, Jitt, we're due for a trading stop on Wishaway," said Captain Northern without looking at his navigator. "Perhaps you'd like to collect your share of the ill-gotten booty of our travels and invest in some real estate there for a retirement."

Jitt's eyes filled with queasy terror. "Wishaway! Captain, the only kind of real estate the Wishaway Colony government would let me buy would be a grave plot!"

"Sounds dreadfully familiar, Jitt. Just what do you do to make all of these worlds so very fond of you?"

"I suppose that since this is such a routine pirate escapade," Jitt said, his tiny eyes downcast, "my excellent intuitive abilities can be ignored. In fact," he continued, blinking as though just hit by a realization, "I do believe they are all cleared up. False alarm, Captain Northern."

"Oh, excellent, Jitt," said Northern, smiling. "Since you now know that the boarding will be a regular tea party, you'll be happy to know that I'm placing you in charge of the detail responsible for retrieving the attilium from the vessel's holds."

Dansen Jitt, for once, was speechless. Tars Northern suspected that it was not from gratitude.

"Suit up, Lieutenant Jitt. I'll maintain the conn. And that's an order, my friend."

"I wish you hadn't thrown away that drink," murmured the little man as he got up to go.

When the raid came upon the Federation Freighter *Ezekiel*, Laura Shemzak was of two minds about it.

First, she admired the precision and the genius of the attack methods. The pi-mercs (known as Star Hounds by the navvies with whom she associated) caught the *Ezekiel* just after its reemergence from Underspace, while the ship's energy fields were still in confused transition. She'd been restlessly pacing on the Observation Deck when the klaxons began to wail, so she got a glimpse of the pinnace sucker-ships darting through the weakened defenses and drilling into airlocks. The pi-merc starship quickly delivered the coup de grace to the *Ezekiel*'s engines, its ray conducted and stepped up by the sucker-ships. Laura picked herself up from the floor, astonished at the technological abilities displayed by a band of renegades.

Second, however, she was mad as hell.

The Lieftian system, holding Jonquil IV, Rameses Base, was just a brief stopover point. Her destination, Shortchild, was perhaps two days down the line, but this freighter was the only conveyance for a week.

The hell with whatever the pi-mercs were stealing. They had shot the boat out from under her! No one did that to Laura Shemzak!

She hauled herself up to where the Observation Deck bubbled out, giving her a vantage point on one of the three sucker-ships. It had bored into an airlock and hung there like a remora gripped to a shark, shimmering softly with residue energy from the field blast that had torn the hell out of the freighter's engines. That airlock was on Level Three, Deck Five, as she recalled. She'd been on the *Ezekiel* for only three days, but she knew it from stem to stern, partly because of her inquisitive nature, but mostly due to her restless energy, which had taken her all through the vessel.

She took the lift to Deck Five.

The whole ship was in pandemonium. Smoke hung in acrid wreaths. Passengers and crew alike darted here and there. Some were sprawled on the floor, but Laura noted immediately that they were not dead. A cursory examination of several revealed the use of stun beams. Apparently the pi-mercs were not as ruthless as they were efficient.

Laura saw the first of the boarders close to the airlock on Deck Five through which they had invaded the starboard side of the freighter. A single gun-wielding pi-merc guarded the entrance to their pinnace.

Laura hung back, skulking in a recessed doorway. One guard was one too many for her plans. She had to act, and act quickly, or her hopes of ever seeing her brother again would fade rapidly from improbable to impossible. She took a quick glance from her hiding place.

By the fit of the guard's silvery, patched suit, she was humanoid and decidedly female. Her hemet's tinted faceplate concealed her features.

Although there was no external sign, the marauding band had to be in contact with some kind of radio. No doubt it was tongue-controlled from behind that polarized visor. Laura rolled back the sleeve of her jump suit.

Then, utilizing the pressure-point code around the blip-ship jack, she peeled back the skin of her forearm and adjusted the radio frequency modulator, a device implanted specifically for blip-ship connection but easily manipulated manually in unattached situations like these. Useful in the field. Tones were born in her ear; she searched the wavelengths. Static gave way to a close-by communications interplay:

". . . located. Blasting operations under way."

"You've got four point two minutes to get your larcenous tails back here," said another voice, a woman's. "Next time, no straw draw. I hate to back up. On top of all this, I'm the only woman among a bunch of tin generals!"

"Captain's orders, Lieutenant Mizel."

Laura took a gamble. She homed in on the frequency and played upon the radio waves with her formidable complement of implanted blip-ship radio array like a maestro, jamming here, tapping there. Utilizing the radio implant in her bicuspids, she spoke just above the subvocal.

"Lieutenant," she said in a pained voice, "wounded . . . just down the corridor . . . help!"

She watched the guard, who raised her energy rifle even as Laura sent the message. "Copy! Who's that?"

Laura remained silent; she fumbled for the door control behind her. The doorway hissed open, revealing a small linen storage closet.

The noise did its job, attracting the guard, who advanced cautiously. Laura had no stun weapon of her own, but she did have her wits. Just as the muzzle of the guard's weapon nosed into view, Laura jammed the radio frequency with high-pitched interference. Another talent of the Radio Lady, she thought grimly. The guard reacted with a jerk. Laura leaped out of her hiding place and grabbed the rifle by its barrel. A martial-arts move later, and the guard was sprawled upside down in the closet. With two deft finger jabs, Laura ensured that the woman was unconscious.

What had the lieutenant said? Four minutes? Not much time.

Laura deftly undid the snap fasteners, valves, and bolts of the suit. The helmet, lifted, disgorged a wealth of blonde, a face of Nordic beauty. "Ride's over, dear

Valkyrie," she said, stripping the suit. "Goddamn, woman, how can you walk?" she added as she stuffed the suit's front with towels to make up for her lack of natural padding. Otherwise, the woman's height about matched, so the suit was a reasonable if somewhat loose fit.

Leaving Lieutenant Mizel tied up and gagged in the closet, Laura picked up the energy rifle and assumed a position by the ravaged airlock.

Within seconds, the first of the pi-merc party returned. "Tried to reach you, Lieutenant. What's up?"

Laura tried to match her memory of the lieutenant's voice. "Radio interference on this end, I think. Where are the others?"

The others were on the heels of their companion. They dragged bags and valises stuffed full of filched treasure.

"Piece of cake, Lieutenant," said one, tossing his bag into the sucker-ship. He had a clipped British accent. "These chaps have been using cardboard for security doors!"

"*Mon dieu!*" cried another, sounding French. "The battle is not over until I am safely returned to my fortress!"

"Get your goddamned European asses in, then," grumped another, "or I'm going to kick 'em there. I'm not going to get myself killed on a milk run."

The squabbling as the party reboarded covered Laura's attempt to remain in the background. She continued her guard duty, even stunning one of the *Ezekiel*'s mates who took it upon himself to make one last effort to stop the pi-mercs. When the party of six was safely ensconced in the pinnace, Laura ducked inside and assumed the only remaining empty seat.

"Excellent," said the Englishman, standing and sealing the lock behind him. "A sterling expedition, gentlemen," he said, taking off his helmet. He had short hair and a plain face.

"Put your goddamned rear end where it goddamned belongs, Wellesley!" growled the grizzled-looking man who had assumed the pilot's position. "We'll have plenty of time for glory back on the *Starbow*."

"Arthur," said the Frenchman, after securing his gravity harness and removing his helmet, "I hope you agree that tactically I am still your better."

"Shut your goddamn flytraps!" said the pilot. "I've got a ship to run."

He turned a stern gaze down to the controls. Deftly manipulating retro-rockets and repulsor beams, he separated the sucker-ship from its prey and pushed out into the void.

"Bloody fine endeavor, George!" said the Englishman as the boat was jockeyed back into space. Laura was sitting by the Frenchman. As all attention was on the ship's maneuvers, she scanned the interior of the sucker-ship. Utilitarian. The only item of possible use in these close quarters was a power gun in the Frenchman's holster.

"Thank you, Arthur," said the crew-cut pilot. "Just a few minutes until docking procedure commences with the *Starbow*. We'll be last back, I'm afraid."

"Lieutenant Mizel," said one of the others, "is your helmet stuck?"

"*Oui!*" said the Frenchman. "You would deprive us of your beauty after such a success?"

"Stuck," Laura murmured. "Would you give me a hand?"

"But of course, mademoiselle," the man replied courteously, reaching up to help undo the seals. Laura leaned over and unsnapped the man's holster, quietly drawing the pistol.

"There!" said the Frenchman. "I do not see any difficulty. Allow me!" Deftly the short man removed the helmet. His smile flip-flopped as he saw the face underneath. "*Sacré bleu,* Lieutenant Mizel. You have changed!"

Laura lifted the pistol's business end to the man's temple. "This isn't on stun anymore, gentlemen," she said, finger tight around the trigger. "And if you excuse the cliché, one false move and this man's brains are going to go EVA."

Heads swiveled. Eyebrows raised.

"Well, I'll be a goddamned mother-loving bastard," said the pilot. He popped a wad of chewing gum in his maw and chomped furiously.

"No great loss, actually," said the Englishman, a huge grin across his face. "I don't know why Mish stuck him in here anyway. Sadistic humor that fellow has. Well then, my lady, I trust you were gentle with our lieutenant."

"She's tied up in a linen closet. She'll have a head-ache when she wakes up, but otherwise she's un-damaged." Laura glared at the pilot. "Now, I mean business, you rancid bunch of pirates. What are your docking procedures? How many other people will be there? Who is your captain? I want to be taken to him as soon as we dock. I have demands to make, and my bargaining tools are your wretched lives."

The words came out quickly and confidently, but, as was often the case in these situations, Laura was simply talking through her hat. The worst moment was just after she jumped face first into things, when she had a moment to consider the implications. She hadn't the faintest idea who these people were, what their ship was like, how warlike they were. . . . Everything she had done was predicated upon one of her insane hunches, hunches that sometimes got her into bizarre situations, like falling in with those No-noses last year during the Mud Festival on Xerxes III.

This was definitely one of those odd situations, and all she could possibly do was bull her way through it, knowing that somehow this would all be to her advan-tage.

The pi-mercs all seemed amused at her request for a conference with their captain, except for the French-man, who looked solemn and thoughtful.

"Well now, ma'am," said the pilot, chewing rapidly on his gum, mouth open. "That should be real fascina-tin' and all, but just what seems to be your problem? Somethin' wrong with stayin' on the *Ezekiel*? We didn't puncture her, and it's not as if there won't be a rescue ship along. Mind you, I'm just wonderin'."

"I have to be someplace in a hurry," said Laura. "I thought I might ask your captain for a ride." Yes, she thought. Promise him money. She could arrange for that.

"Ask Captain Tars Northern for a ride, eh?" The pilot grinned facetiously. "Pretty girl like you shouldn't ask horny bastards like Northern for a ride."

"I mean it," she said angrily, pressing the gun harder against the Frenchman's skull. "If I have to show it bloodily, I will be most happy to."

"Mademoiselle, please," said the Frenchman, but with no trace of fear.

"Too much like the old shrew back home, eh, Boney?" said the one he'd addressed as Arthur. "I believe, old boy, that you've met another Waterloo!" The fellow laughed uproariously.

"I really don't see what's so funny," Laura said through clenched teeth.

"Oh, you will, ma'am," said the pilot. "You sure will! Now, if you'll excuse me, I've got to get back to work. And be careful there with old Boney. He's a slippery one!"

Laura Shemzak frowned.

Something was definitely wrong here, besides the fact that she was taking this one unknown step at a time.

And the worst of it was, she seemed to be the only one who had no idea what that something was.

Chapter Seven

THE pinnace communicated with the mother ship, clearing its redocking with the necessary codes.

"Yep, you must be one tough cookie to put Kat Mizel away like that," the pilot—whom the others called variously "Patton" or "George"—commented as the computer went on automatic and the *Starbow*'s tractor guided the pinnace to home port. "You independent? Or are you a Feddy?"

"I'm independent now, but to be perfectly up front, I am a highly trained officer of the Federation, and the only reason I'm associating with scum of your low caliber is that you have something that I need. I'm a reasonable sort, so—" She broke off, staring at the vuplates. The *Starbow* was unlike any interstellar vessel Laura had seen before.

The pilot noticed the direction of his passenger's gaze. "Aha, I see the old *Starbow* has caught your eye. A beauty, isn't she?"

The main body of the starship was sleek and silvery and beautiful. It glowed with a multitextured radiance. More remarkable, however, were the thick spokes radiating from the hub, ending in various jewel shapes, shimmering bezels set in a gigantic pendant hung around the neck of night.

Patton grinned. "Nope. Just don't make 'em like they used to." His eyes gleamed strangely with some private joke. "And they probably never will again."

"I've never seen the like in any catalog back home," Laura admitted. "Is it of alien manufacture?"

"You'll have to ask the captain."

"Yeah. I'm looking forward to that," Laura said, redirecting her attention back where it belonged: on her captives, lest they try something.

All six of them were amazingly calm, even the one to whose temple she held the pistol. They all sat patiently, waiting as the hangar deck of the *Starbow* opened amidships, a hungry mouth awaiting a morsel of food.

Laura Shemzak was worried. God knew she'd been in stranger situations, and certainly more violent ones. But now, with this strange crew, and all this quiet, she was a little unnerved. Also, she realized, all those times before she was responsible only for herself and the Federation's wishes.

Now she had elected to be responsible for the rescue of someone she truly cared about—Cal, her brother. The thought of him brought back her resolve. As crazy and strange as all this seemed, it was the only way she had any hope of seeing Cal again.

The pinnace fitted snugly into its slot, with barely a clang.

A voice erupted through the cabin. "Locks cycled. Ready for deboarding."

"Yes," said Arthur Wellesley. "But are they ready for what will be deboarding?"

"I think they should be," Laura said. "Notify your captain that I would very much like to have him waiting outside, in person, for a short discussion."

"Sure thing, lady," said George Patton. "I'm sure that Tars is gonna want to meet you just as soon as possible."

The docking bay was spacious. Their footsteps echoed as they walked along the floor, which was marked brightly with strange patterns and hieroglyphics. Laura hung back behind the pi-mercs, pistol trained steadily upon the base of the Frenchman's head.

Captain Tars Northern waited for them, leaning against the railing of a upper gangway. Beside him stood a slight, querulous-looking man and a tall, stooped individual in a lab smock and a voluminous purple bow tie.

Captain Tars Northern held a bottle of brandy in one hand. He saluted the new arrivals and tippled a few swallows. "Welcome back, my comrades. Our new arrival, I salute you. Hail and well met, O wandering star lass!"

"Captain, really," the man to his left said, eyes darting nervously about. "Don't you think a little decorum—"

"Oh, get your prissy little nose outa my business, Jitt," said the captain. "The doctor here is monitoring me and my condition, and my condition is just fine, thank you. Isn't it, Dr. Mish?"

The man in the lab smock smiled wanly, examining a small machine held in one hand. "You are reaching your hour's consumption limit, Captain."

"Oh hell, I'm celebrating," the captain said. Although his words were spoken overcarefully, they were not slurred, and his eyes were bright and aware, his feet steady. He looked down at the visitor fondly. "It's not every day that we get a Feddy agent come to call."

Laura could not believe her eyes. "You're drunk!" she said. "I have the life of one of your crew members at the end of a cocked gun, and you're boozing?"

Captain Northern grinned. "Yo ho ho, and a bottle of rum, my dear!" He leaned on his doctor's shoulder. "We must keep up appearances for our Feddy Friends, mustn't we. Yes indeed. You"— he pointed a finger at her, chuckling—"have done me a most enormous favor, dear lady!"

Laura glanced around suspiciously, expecting some sort of trick. But she could sense nothing wrong, even with her interior sensors clicked up full. "I have demands to make, Captain!" she shouted. "Do not joke with me! I want to bargain the life of this man for a large favor.''

Dr. Mish shook his head sadly. Captain Northern whooped. ''Oh dear, you mean you would really blow off the head of Napoleon Bonaparte?''

Laura blinked. She'd heard that name before—long, long before.

''You need not worry, mademoiselle,'' said Napoleon Bonaparte. ''They'll just reassemble me. I'm just a robot, you see.''

Dr. Mish signaled.

Napoleon Bonaparte ducked with amazing speed. Arthur Wellesley, Duke of Wellington, was the one to take the full force of the blast. It took Wellington's right arm off, but his left arm knocked the gun from Laura's hand before she could pull the trigger again. Bonaparte was on his feet, but Laura agilely dodged his attempt to grab her. She leaped for the gun lying on the floor, but somehow Bonaparte's arm snagged onto her ankle. Automatically twisting as she fell, she managed to wrench free and land on her hands and feet.

Robots! Of course! It all fell together, even Kat Mizel's complaints about ''tin generals.'' The main body of the pi-merc boarding party must have been robots—much safer!

But she had to get that gun, she knew—there was no way she could threaten anything or anybody and get her way with her bare hands.

''Would you things get on with it?'' she heard Captain Northern yell. ''Grab her before she does anything silly!''

Of course. If she could just get to the captain . . .

She dodged one of the robots and struck out for her destination. But the Bonaparte robot grabbed her from behind in an amazing jump. It put Laura in an astonishingly strong half nelson before she could get anywhere near Northern.

''Jolly good show, Boney,'' said the duke, wires trailing from his shoulder socket. ''Did the admiral who beat you at Trafalgar teach you that?''

Chapter Eight

"STICK her in the brig. We'll interrogate her later," Captain Northern said, smiling at the word "interrogate." "We've got to supervise the unloading of the other ships."

By now three of the robots were restraining Laura; she had flailed about powerfully, so Patton and another robot had aided Napoleon.

"Captain," said the tall, white-haired man beside him, examining his clipboard. "My sensors show that the young lady is veritably riddled with artificial materials of an intensely sophisticated variety. I strongly suggest, if you're going to incarcerate the young lady before any discussions with her, that a heavy guard be placed . . . or even that she be medicinally rendered unconscious."

"A cyborg. Perhaps with a few tricks up her sleeves, you say. Curiouser and curiouser." He capped his bottle and slipped it into the doctor's voluminous side pocket. "Enough of that. Tell me, Doctor, are there any signs of anything dangerous inside her?"

"No, I've checked that. Further, more detailed information can be derived at a later date."

"All I want," Laura said, "is passage to Shortchild. Take me there, and I'll spare your lives! Ouch!" she said as Patton increased pressure on one of her arms.

"Feisty little thing. Jitt, take care of her. She can keep her consciousness as long as she's good. Post guards. I'll speak to her when the ships are unloaded."

"But time is of the essence," Laura cried, desperation causing her to lose control. "I have to get to that base to get my blip-ship!"

Captain Northern had turned to depart, but he halted in his tracks. "Doctor, did I hear her say blip-ship? Do you mean the XT line, young lady?"

"Hmm," said the doctor. "That would explain the biomech additions to her nervous and skeletal systems."

Captain Northern clapped his hands, immensely pleased. "Young lady, I will talk to you, then, within the hour!"

The "brig" turned out to be a spartan cabin, with reinforced bulkheads and door. After searching her for concealed weapons, the robots tossed her in and locked the door. She kicked the small bunk furiously then lay down with a wail that died into a whimper.

So what was she going to do now, she wondered. Everything was in the captain's hands, and he appeared to be raving mad . . . or at least a drunk. Why did his crew follow him, take his orders? What kind of power did he have over them?

"What did you say your name was?" a voice asked through a speaker. Laura recognized the soft whiny quality; it was the man the others had called Dansen Jitt.

"Is this part of the vaunted interrogation?" Laura asked contemptuously. Jitt had hung back far behind them as they navigated the corridors and lifts that eventually led to this cold, sterile room, carefully training a stun gun on her. She had pegged him as a coward immediately, what with his nervous eyes, his tremulous mouth. Nonetheless, there was a shy, unique beauty to his face, a grace to his gestures and movements that she found attractive, now that she recalled them.

She took a curious comfort in the sound of his voice.

After all, Jitt didn't seem to particularly relish his duties as guard; he certainly didn't seem to want her hurt.

Besides, she thought, I shouldn't be nasty to him. I should pump him for information. Maybe I can get an idea of what the captain has in mind for me—and maybe I can find out how to make some kind of deal with him. He seems awfully interested in the fact that I'm a blip-ship pilot.

"Oh no, no, the captain makes jokes sometimes, strange jokes, and that was one of them. Sometimes, though, he is serious when he seems to be joking, and that puts things quite out of whack."

"I am Laura Shemzak," she said in a softer voice. Volume and demands would get her nowhere now. "Your captain . . . is he mentally deranged?"

Jitt laughed. "Oh, you might think so, and he would love to admit it, if that would throw you off. Let's just say that the mind of Captain Tars Northern has its demons, and it has its angels . . . and it most certainly has a clown or two. I shouldn't be talking to you, but I just can't imagine why you'd want to get on board this crazy ship. Sometimes I think I'd like to get off!"

"Didn't you hear what I said out there? I just need a ride. I can pay well, and it's really very important."

"Well, you should talk to the captain about that, not me."

"He seemed strangely unmoved by the loss of one of his crew members. She was human, or I couldn't have knocked her out the way I did," said Laura, hoping to keep the little man talking. He certainly seemed the talkative type, and she could use all the information she could get.

"Oh yes, Lieutenant Kat Mizel. I don't suppose that, you being a Feddy, you'd comprehend. But you see, Mizel and Northern had a bit of a bond. Captain Northern got drunk on Rook's World two months ago and woke up married to Lieutenant Mizel. They have a year's contract, but Kat had been hounding him about making it longer, about having children, and God knows what else. I think Captain Northern is actually quite relieved that today's events are going to allow the remaining ten months of the contract expire without close proximity to the lieutenant."

"Marriage, yes, of course," Laura said, smiling despite herself. "My brother and I . . . we watched ancient films about marriage. Cal found the most bizarre books. . . . It is a very funny state, marriage."

"I wish I could have convinced Kat Mizel of that. We've had more conflict in this boat the past two months than the Federation Fleet experienced when the Jaxdrons invaded! The captain, for all he swears, is just not suited for even temporary matrimonial bliss."

"Then the rumors are true. The rite still exists on some of the more barbaric colony worlds. I thought the tales in the tabloids were manufactured. Are you married, Dansen Jitt?"

"I will admit to a few wives on various worlds, yes. But you mentioned a brother. I didn't know you Feddies had brothers and sisters. I thought they just stirred up some zygotes in a womb vat, added salt to flavor, and disgorged children into the maw of society."

Laura could not help but smile mischievously. "The government goofed. We found out, you see. We . . . love each other. We have sworn loyalty to one another."

"The Feddy Friends must not approve of that," Dansen Jitt commented.

"There's nothing they can do. They need us."

"Right. Blip-ship pilot. Marvelous. I've never met one. You seem reasonably normal. Is that what your brother does as well?"

"No."

Dansen Jitt, unfrightened, proved conversationally convivial. Twenty minutes later, though Laura had learned little about the *Starbow* beyond the fact that it was an independent vessel plying its mercenary and piratical trade on the rim of Federation space, she did find out much about Dansen Jitt—he seemed to adore talking about himself, and he did so wittily and fluently. As though the speech was practiced, thought Laura, and Jitt was eager for an audience.

The state of being human had always been a confusing experience since the dawn of consciousness, Laura knew. But life in the thirty-first century Old Dating System, 734.34 in the N.D.S., was particularly vexing because of shadowy areas developing between the "human" and "nonhuman." Indeed, on certain worlds one could opt out of the dilemma totally by literally transforming to the alien. Xenoforming the process was called, and it was a development created more than five hundred years before when colonists seeking a planet to make their own learned that it was much less hassle and infinitely less expensive to genetically engineer themselves to an environment instead of terraforming a non-Earth-standard planet.

Dansen Jitt was born on a planet in the Antares sector, a world called Changeit in Neogalactic. His colony was one of the first to adopt xenoforming, adapting to fit to the ecology of a world rich with a different chemical structure from Earth standard. However, after thousands of humans had adjusted, something cataclysmic happened to their sensibilities. It was voted, through their democratic government, to change back to Earth Human Standard and travel the course of terraforming. The transition, though costly and difficult, was a success, and Changeit became one of the most successful new worlds, rich in everything. But its inhabitants were somehow different for their double change; tradition said the Changed had seen something in their New Reality that so terrorized them that their choice was either to return to their previous state or destroy themselves. As a result, their descendants owned unusual near-psychic talents . . . and tended toward a constant state of low-level fear and paranoia.

Dansen Jitt had been the son of a merchant. Early in his life he had discovered his knack for accuracy in statistical odds—without the benefit of actual hard statistics. The facts, he told Laura, would pop into his head at the most erratic moments. He found that he could use this "talent" to his best advantage in the casinos of the Anarchy Worlds, and for a long time went on boom-and-bust cycles of wealth. Occasional

deep gambling debts forced him into a life of periodic
crime, which he hated because of his overwhelming
cowardice. He soon became persona non grata on many
worlds.

However, just last year, he had met a remarkable
fellow in a particularly seedy dive on Marshton IV.

"I was down on my funds, but statistically I was hot
and the stuff was pouring into me as the dice rolled on
the spinning cards. Shaksa we were playing, and one of
the heavy losers was a military-looking guy who drank
like he had an empty leg.

"After the game he asked me to buy him a drink.
'Jitt,' he says, 'how'd you like to make some real money
and get the opportunity to enjoy it without Authority
breathing down your backside?'

"He explained he was a captain of the most wonderful starship in the universe. 'Now, mind you, we do
need funds, so occasionally we knock off the odd Federation vessel, or hire our services to the wealthy. Nothing
too dangerous, and I distinguish something in you that
could make it even less dangerous.'

"Well, he couldn't have come at a better time. I had
almost nowhere to go. I was even a criminal on
Changeit. So I agreed.

"Of course, Northern was lying through his teeth
about what the *Starbow* truly does. . . . But if you stick
around for any length of time, I suppose you'll discover
that fact readily enough."

Laura supposed she would have to stick around for a
time; she didn't want to try to escape, because the
Starbow was her hope for getting to Shortchild quickly.

Laura attempted to probe for more information, but
at that point Dansen Jitt was interrupted and notified
that the captain was ready for an audience with the captive, and would he and the robot guards kindly lead her
to the galley, where a modest dinner was under way?

This suited Laura very well, for not only did she wish
to bargain with the captain of this weird boat; she was
also quite hungry.

Chapter Nine

THE galley proved more of a stateroom. Laura had been on a great many starships in her four years alternating between Intelligence and blip-ship testing, but she had never seen anything like this on any of them. She had seen rooms like this in some of the old movies that Cal had dredged up from the substorage basements. What age did those films depict? Oh yes, "Victorian" it was called.

"Greetings, Laura Shemzak," said Captain Tars Northern from behind a large cut-glass goblet of red wine. "Please have a seat. Soup will be served quite soon."

The chamber was lined with dark wood paneling. A chandelier, curlings of steel to which glass and light clung like Boxinian fire bees, hung over a long walnut table. Dansen Jitt guided Laura to a high-backed wooden chair opposite the captain and the other two diners, Dr. Mish and a man Laura did not recognize. After seating her, Jitt signaled the robots to remain, but sat beside Laura, which signaled to her his trust.

The gesture was not lost on Captain Northern. He smiled broadly. "Mr. Cromwell," he ordered a robot servant, "would you pour our guest some wine?"

To one side of the captain sat the ever vigilant Dr.

Mish, gripping his sensor board, still wearing a lab
smock. To the other sat a dark, intense young man who
was looking at Laura as though he possessed X-ray vision. Laura allowed the wine to be poured, but did not
touch it.

Dansen Jitt held a finger in the air as though remembering something. "The young lady and I had a very
splendid conversation, and I can vouch for her intelligence and apparent sincerity."

"May I introduce my first mate, Mr. Arkm Thur,"
the captain said, after acknowledging Dansen Jitt's
testimonial with a nod. Despite the presence of wine, he
seemed entirely sober; he seemed much more solemn,
now, his aspect bereft of its previous animated humor.
But his tone remained slightly droll.

Laura, impatient even with this brief ceremony,
decided to take a more direct tack.

"I want you to take me to Shortchild. I can arrange
for recompense, Captain. And I promise to strike this
kidnapping from your Federation record."

"Kidnapping?" Northern said, almost spewing wine
all over the table. "We didn't raid the *Ezekiel* to steal an
arrogant, troublesome bitch!"

"Might I remind you, Captain, that even verbal
assault is an offense. I have a good memory, and this
will be reported."

The first mate scowled, shook his head. "She seems
to be falling back on the mind-screw methodologies of
Federation officers, Captain. Sound and fury, signify-
ing nothing."

The captain nodded and said, "Now, can we get to
some realistic discussion? Being pragmatists, we naturally wonder why we should even allow you to breathe
our air after your frightful display!" Captain Northern
hid a smile behind a napkin and coughed before resum-
ing. "My first mate would be happy to be in charge of
ejecting you into raw space. Wouldn't you, Arkm?"

First Mate Thur said, "It would be a pleasure, Captain. Lieutenant Mizel and I were very close."

This is all just too much, Laura thought, losing control of her temper.

"Would you cut this goddamned mealy-mouthed crap!" she said, standing up and spilling her wine in the process. "You're not scaring me. If you want your over-ripe wife back, Northern, you can go back and get her! That freighter's gonna be just where you left it."

"We do not believe in suicide!" Northern said, matching her glare with his own. He then turned a scathing glance on Dansen Jitt.

"And just what kind of money am I going to have to pay you to get me where I want to go?" Laura finished.

"Ah! Now we get to where we want to be," said the captain. "Dr. Mish, just what is the going rate these days for passenger transport aboard the *Starbow*?"

Dr. Mish began to punch buttons on his board.

"No, wait a moment. We have no great need of money, have we, Mr. Thur?"

"Our treasury is quite healthy in all manner of currency—particularly FedEmp currency, Captain."

"So. Laura, let me ask you a question. I understand that this little pangalactic jaunt is not official Federation business. I heard you tell Mr. Jitt that you are seeking your brother. Who and what is your brother, and have you any idea of where he may be?"

So he *had* been monitoring her conversation with Jitt—she had thought there was something odd when the little man stayed to talk. Still, there was no reason not to tell them about Cal. "My brother is Cal Shemzak. He was captured by the Jaxdrons on a recent raid."

Dr. Mish blinked. "Shemzak. I knew I'd heard that name. Cal Shemzak! Of course. Your brother . . . Cal Shemzak is a Federation physicist, specializing in . . ." His words trailed off as a manic gleam came to his eyes.

Captain Northern turned his attention back to Laura. "You are a blip-ship pilot, according to your own statements and our good doctor's sensor readings. You have a great many implants—your body must be one mass of scar tissue." More quietly, he said, "Is that the reason for your drab coverall?"

Laura smiled. "Federation surgery is quite sophisticated, Captain. I have a minimum of scar tissue. Do you want me to prove it to you?" One hand rested on the

Velcro closure of her jump suit.

Captain Tars Northern raised his eyebrows. "Sounds interesting, but no, we'll take your word, I think."

Laura took her hand away from the fastener and relaxed fractionally, sipping her wine.

Northern continued, "Our doctor here would very much like to meet your brother. Apparently he is familiar with Shemzak's work. I've never encountered a blip-ship, wouldn't mind having one on board for a while. Therefore I think we can strike a small bargain, Laura Shemzak." He leaned forward with a smile that, if it weren't so hard, might be termed "mischievous."

Laura well understood Northern's interest in blip-ships. The XT program was a top-secret Federation project. So far none of the Free Worlds had anything resembling the small, ultrafast, surface/system/Underspace vessels. Any information concerning the structure of one would be valuable on the black market; an actual blip-ship itself would be priceless.

By bringing a blip-ship on board the *Starbow*, she would be committing that most heinous act against the Friendhood: treason.

On the other hand, she couldn't care less about the Friendhood. Loyalty to them, after all, was programmed, knee-jerk stuff, nothing earned or valuable, like her respect, her love for her brother.

And besides, who said she would have to keep faith with a bunch of pirates if, once she got good solid blip-ship alloy around her pretty tail, she simply thumbed her nose at Captain Tars Almighty Northern and vamoosed?

She called for a refill for her wineglass. "Sure, Captain. Why not?" She grabbed a napkin and stuffed one corner into the neck of her jump suit. "Now, did you say some food was on its way? I'm hungry as a Denebian frogbeast popping out of hibernation!"

Chapter Ten

So, Laura thought, again my intuition was right. I have landed in a peculiar situation, but it looks as though I've got a ride.

Since the deal was struck, she felt no compulsion to be anything but herself. As the soup was served, she fell silent and observed the interplay of the unusual personalities around her, honestly curious about what kind of people banded together to become pirates and mercenaries. Since her own course in life had been mostly plotted, it was difficult for her to understand an autonomous group of intelligent, if bizarre, individuals.

After the soup, a savory concoction of broth and a variety of vegetation Laura had never seen before, two more crew members joined the party.

The two had helped unload the loot captured from the stricken *Ezekiel*. Whether or not they had actually participated in the raid they did not say; but from the looks of them, Laura surmised that they had every bit as much spunk as Lieutenant Kat Mizel.

Laura took an immediate shine to Midshipman Gemma Naquist. She wore red hair cut in a no-nonsense bob over a face that was at least Celtic, if not Irish. Bright blue eyes above freckles and a pert nose shone with intelligence. Her body, in a gray uniform, was willowy but firm. She seemed to own all of the self-confidence that Laura feared she lacked. Older by at least half a decade, Gemma was someone Laura would like to talk to.

But Gemma Naquist, like her counterpart, Midshipman Silver Zenyo, hardly gave the dinner guest notice.

Laura despised Silver Zenyo on the spot.

Zenyo was the kind of creature, Laura assumed, who lived off the metaphorical blood of others. Her hair was a beautiful, well-kept cloud of chiffon. Her creamy features were no doubt surgically softened from their true harpy nature. She affected a frilled blouse and bright red trim to her uniform. And worst of all, she was painted . . . she wore makeup . . . something you only saw these days on the more decadent colonies like Wonderwhat and Heidi-Ho. Her body, hands, and features moved in a manner calculated to manipulate the sexual interest of males, and only Dr. Mish seemed unaffected by her presence. The stench of her perfume wafted across the table, smelling to Laura like swamp gas.

But her power was not merely in manipulation; beneath everything else, Laura sensed a deep strength. Beneath a playful half smile there also moved a mystery that intrigued Laura, despite her intense initial reaction of distaste.

"And my attilium?" Dr. Mish asked, interrupting the staccato report given by Midshipman Naquist.

"I'm sorry, Doctor," said Naquist, "but there was no sign of attilium. The boarding parties did double-check."

"But I detected something on my sensors," Dr. Mish said bemusedly. "Oh dear oh dear. Shontill is not going to be pleased. I could have sworn . . . Oh well, it must have been a misreading. Some Federation impulse engines are using new power nodes. Still, Shontill will be upset."

"Just keep a leash on that ungodly beast," Silver Zenyo said, her nose turned up disgustedly. "The last time he had a tantrum, he traumatized my poor Bickle!"

"Shontill would rather *eat* Bickle, I think," Gemma said, deadpan.

"Gemma, how could you even suggest such a thing?" She turned long-lashed eyes toward Captain Northern. "Tars, you would never permit such an atrocity, would you?"

Northern shrugged noncommittally. "It's an alien-eat-alien universe, Midshipman."

Laura slurped the last of her soup, and burped. "Alien, huh? You mean human-type or the real McCoy?" she said, emphasizing on purpose her boorish qualities to annoy Silver.

Silver Zenyo gave the newcomer a disgusted look. "My goodness, at least Shontill excuses himself when he makes rude noises."

"Is there something more coming, or are you all on some strange type of diet?" Laura asked, frowning at Silver Zenyo.

"Oh yes, of course," said Dr. Mish, pressing buttons. "My lads are quite prompt, but I neglected to give the proper orders."

"The robots' names," said Laura, "Are awfully familiar."

"Yes," Captain Northern said as the robot called Oliver Cromwell rolled a cart into the room. "A conceit of our dear Michael Mish."

Dr. Mish nodded. "I've been experimenting with artificial persona overlays in robots, and my latest bunch have been based on famous military leaders of Earth." Laura nodded as she remembered her history lessons.

Dinner was an excellent dish of processed algae-beef and soy-noodles, flavored by odd but pleasing spices. Laura ate with zest, occasionally splattering her bib or herself with gravy in the vigor of her appetite.

"Were you born in a barn, girl?" Silver Zenyo said, alarmed. "Really, Captain, it's bad enough we have to transport a Feddy agent. Must we tolerate her at supper?"

"All that fluffy hair clogging your ears?" Laura said, the faint drawl in her accent purposefully pronounced for maximum annoyance. She licked her thumb, popping it out of her mouth with a vaguely obscene sound. "I'm a damned important addition to your comfy little crew. Aren't I, Northern?"

She could feel her self-confidence and cockiness returning. This is gonna be okay, she told herself.

"We'll see about that, Laura Shemzak," said the captain, all traces of levity gone from his manner. Laura felt something of the true power of his personality and immediately lost her appetite. "Let's hope so, for all our sakes."

Captain Northern picked up a knife and sliced a piece of pseudo-beef that could have easily been cut with his fork.

Chapter Eleven

THE foil flashed, neatly riposting the blow. Steel shivered. Chivon Lasster retreated, and the man with whom she dueled advanced, his blade of energy shedding sparks as it touched the metal of her weapon.

Suddenly her opponent executed a complicated series of movements. Lasster's foil was torn from her grasp, clattering off to the other side of the room. The fencer lunged, his translucent blade cutting neatly through her chest.

Chivon looked down. "Does it have to be so realistic?" she asked.

"If you are to learn the true art of fencing, you must feel the attendant fear, yes," the figure before her said. In a twinkling, his weapon vanished. He stepped back, his body growing more opaque as it neared the field source. "I trust you enjoyed your lesson today, Friend Lasster?" the Computer Companion said.

A trifle shaken, Chivon Lasster went to get a drink. "I don't think that's the correct word, Andrew. Very good exercise, though."

"And I don't think that's the right after-exercise refreshment," the CompComp admonished. "Would you care for a discussion of the effects of the C_2H_5OH

molecule upon the human nervous system, to say nothing of—"

"No!" Chivon Lasster said curtly, tossing back a finger of contraband Xorfrost brandy. "Spare me, please."

The CompComp glimmered softly. "You are still troubled, Chivon Lasster. The readings are plain enough. I thought we had discussed this matter fully, utilizing the specific focusing processes that usually work so well for an individual of your temperament."

She poured another, larger, portion of brandy.

"The other aspects of this business," Andrew continued, sitting down and folding his long fingers together in a professorial manner. "Zarpfrin . . . Zarpfrin's machinations. The implant. The suicidal mission. The Jaxdron. Laura Shemzak. All this would not truly trouble you except for certain associations, would it?"

She let the sting of the brandy nip her tongue, slide down her throat, warm her stomach. "Say it. Go ahead and say it, then," she sighed. "I've not been stingy with the use of the name. I freely admit that I am still deeply troubled by Tars Northern, that our partnership in the days of the project and his . . . his traitorous behavior, his abandonment of loyalty . . ." Her words trailed off as she realized how much emotion she was giving them. "Tars Northern, Andrew, as you will no doubt find if you care to take the effort to check your data banks, was and no doubt still is a larcenous, unprincipled thief, scoundrel, and . . . well, I haven't a thesaurus on hand, but all the rest of the synonyms apply. He goes against everything that we stand for in this state . . . all the principles of behavior and value that for once have united humanity in a coherent program for progress and advancement within a free and just framework!" She took another sip of her drink. The words came so easily . . . too easily. Mere recitation.

"Tars Northern was also your copilot. You and he cohabited for a time. You created a few zygotes together for the state, did you not?" Andrew said, and there was a touch of the sardonic in his voice: unusual for a machine, or a projection of a machine, or whatever the hell he was, Chivon thought. "An expert manipulator of your sensory capabilities, Tars Northern. A tireless and kind and virile—"

"Manipulator!" Chivon interrupted loudly. "That's the word. Captain Tars Northern definitely knew his way around machinery, software or hardware. He knew so much more about the *Starbow* than I could have ever dreamed of knowing . . . and he learned it so quickly. Dr. Mish would say something that . . . that was like an alien nonsense language, and Tars had but to ask a few questions and he could assimilate it. Even," she said, pouring more brandy, "even when he was drinking." She looked at the amber liquid in the glass. "He was manipulating me when he promised that we were a team, always, as long as there was a *Starbow* to co-pilot."

"But surely that agreement terminated with the somewhat spectacular cessation of the project, when he began seeing what was happening to the other AI ships. And you were so involved at the time with your work with the Friends, your political connections through Zarpfrin, the project administrator. When Northern made his decision, is it not true that you were on the other side of Earth?"

"I never thought he would betray the Federation. Why was I so blind, Andrew, why did I not take precautions? Zarpfrin specifically requested such, and his wisdom fell upon deaf ears. Why?"

"Because," said the holo-projection in a soft voice, "you were in love then with Tars Northern, as you are now."

"No!" Chivon shrieked. She hurled the glass at the specter, spilling liquid over the carpet. The glass went through the holo-projection and bounced off the seat's padding. Her face contorted. "No!" And then she caught herself. She straightened and looked at Andrew. "Such a word is not used by CompComps, Andrew. At least not in such a context. And if you see vestiges of such an illusory and decadent emotion in your fleshly charge, is it not your duty to bring to bear the proper deconditioning procedures?''

"Proper initial analysis is always necessary, Friend Lasster,'' replied Andrew in an even voice.

"You say that very glibly, Andrew. Too glibly. I think that we should talk further, or perhaps I should have your memory chips scanned for faults. Now let me ask you Andrew, my trusted CompComp''—she said the words through clenched teeth—"how do you know that word?''

Before Andrew could answer, the communicator in Chivon Lasster's apartment chimed. Chivon flicked it on. The vu-screen revealed the image of Overfriend Zarpfrin.

"I want you back at headquarters, immediately,'' he told her. "We have a very interesting development with this Laura Shemzak business. The *Ezekiel* was attacked by a group of Star Hounds. Agent Shemzak infiltrated the Star Hound vessel. However, a pirate was taken captive. She's being transported to Earth. We need to plan our methods of interrogation . . . and you need a full debriefing.''

"On my way,'' Lasster said.

Star Hounds! she thought. Why, that could mean that—

She ran for the door, forgetting to turn off the communicator, forgetting to turn off her computer.

The projection of the CompComp that Chivon Lasster called Andrew watched her leave.

"I know the word, Friend Chivon Lasster,'' he said solemnly, standing up. "I know the word, because I know you.''

He turned off his extension, and the ghostly holograph instantly disappeared.

Chapter Twelve

NAVIGATOR Dansen Jitt had calculated a two-day run to Shortchild. After an examination by Dr. Michael Mish, Laura was granted limited run of the starship's facilities. When she was not assigned to blip-ship duty, Laura often had sophisticated weaponry fitted inside her, useful when on assignment in the field. Thankfully, the weapons had been removed in preparation for her attachment to the XT Mark Nine; God knew what the Star Hounds would have done if they'd discovered that kind of stuff hidden inside her.

When she'd asked how limited her wanderings would be, Captain Northern had been curt but specific. "Anywhere you can go without an indentipad." Indentipads, it seemed, were implanted in the palms of the crew, especially coded to give access to certain areas of the ship. This aroused Laura's curiosity no end. Why would sections be restricted? Laura rapidly discovered that, besides many rooms in the main body of the *Starbow*, she also could not enter the radii that extended to the peculiar pods surrounding the craft.

Since the crew people obliged her questions only at the meals she shared with them, and then only begrudgingly, Laura grew rapidly bored and decided that she would occupy her spare time by finding a way to enter a prohibited area.

The area she chose turned out to be the quarters of Shontill, and she finally gained entry during one of its sleep cycles. Had anyone explained to Laura what Shontill was like during a sleep cycle, she might have been more than satisfied with her ennui.

In her days working for the Federated Empire, Laura Shemzak had encountered her share of intelligent alien life, to say nothing of the bizarrely unintelligent. Life in the Milky Way galaxy, it seemed, was every bit as plentiful and richly varied as early human visionaries had dreamed it would be, even before the first man set foot upon the moon. Almost every star system had life on one of its primaries, carbon- or silicon-based, unicellular or exoskeletoned or the practically limitless varieties of possibility.

Laura had seen the Eyebats of Rigel III, danced to the music of Beta Centauri's Drumbeasts, and shared the Carbon Dioxide Sacrament with the MindLungs from Betelgeuse IV. But she had never before encountered the likes of the alien that the crew of the *Starbow* called Shontill.

Opening the door was child's play. Laura had selected the door—situated in the port quarter, out of the way of the crew and their industrious robots—because it felt different. She scanned it, went back to her cabin, assumed a lotus position, and tranced out her detail analysis. She then peeled back the skin from her forearm and adjusted her blip-ship radio connection circuits. When she returned to the door, she flipped back her finger tabs, making metal-to-metal contact and issuing the code that unlocked the door.

It hissed open.

Laura stepped in.

The first thing that hit her was the smell: a trace of sulfur in a rich broth of oxygen and other gases. Though the mix was obviously not harmful to human beings, it was definitely not Earth standard.

The room was dimly lit by lamps scattered about beneath vines and foliage. After her spartan cabin and the bare hallways, Laura felt as though she had stepped into the hydroponics section . . . but she knew that these

were like no plants normally grown for food and gas ex-
change on a starship. The red-purplish leaves stirred
with her passage, as though cringing away from her.
Something rustled in the darkness above her head.

A sense of wrongness raised goose bumps on her skin.
The room had an oval portal opening onto other rooms
with different-colored lights, like a tunnel through a
floral womb. The scents of many flowers wafted in the
air.

In the next room the walls glowed with a faint
phosphorescence, like some sea cave. One side of the
room was occupied by a large tank. Bubbles drifted up
languidly. Seaweed-like fronds rooted in a murky mud
drifted over a large form floating in the liquid.

Curiosity drew her closer.

The form stretched out two meters horizontally. It
had a roughly humanoid shape, though definite features
could not be discerned because of a mucous cocoon that
surrounded it. Fascinated, Laura looked closer into the
tank. Was that a head? she wondered. Just what was
Captain Tars Northern keeping in here, anyway?

Suddenly Laura Shemzak found herself staring eye to
something like an eye. Despite her training, she froze,
hypnotized.

A long tentacle erupted from the liquid and curled
around Laura's midsection, lifting her off the deck. As
she fruitlessly struggled, the thing pushed itself up, and
its head reared over the edge of the tank. Razor-sharp
fangs glimmered in the soft light.

"Erughrhghhhgh," came a gurgling noise that
sounded like a combination of anger and hunger.

Laura, to her extreme shame, realized that she was
screaming.

The tentacle shook her, squeezing the breath from
her.

"Who . . . are . . . you?" the thing asked in a froggy
voice, bringing Laura closer to its face, which looked
like something from the ooze of an alien sea. Its features
were shifting, rearranging into something almost human.

It was Laura's turn to emit nonsense sounds. She felt

as though her eyes were about to pop from their sockets.

"Perhaps if you released your grip a tad, Shontill," someone said from the shadows, "she might be able to answer you."

A light snapped on.

Instantly filmy green nictitating eyelids dropped over the alien's eyes.

"Well, go ahead, Shontill," said Captain Tars Northern. "Eat her if you want, but your digestive tract, heavy-duty as it may be, is going to have some problem getting around some of the junk the Federation stuck inside her!"

"You . . . are . . . fortunate," the alien said. Its tentacle dragged Laura closer, and its foul breath washed over her. "I . . . awake . . . famished." In contempt, it tossed the woman head over heels toward Tars Northern. Northern nimbly stepped out of the way, allowing Laura to land, sprawling, in a bunch of plants.

"Are you all right?" Tars Northern asked, helping her out.

Laura was *not* all right. She was terrified, trained reactions overwhelmed by her unexpected encounter with the giant alien. She grabbed Northern and clung to him, gasping for air. He was strong and warm, and he did not push her away. He patted her back softly, stroked her fine short hair, comforting her.

Abruptly she realized what she was doing.

She pushed him away. "Get your stinking hands off me!" she shrieked, still not in control of her breathing. She backed to the wall, staring suspiciously at both Northern and the newly awakened alien.

"I suspect, Shontill, that the inorganic parts of her aren't the only tough bits," said Tars Northern in a maddeningly casual way. "As long as you are up, Dr. Mish wants to speak to you."

The alien had . . . changed. Its tentacles more closely resembled arms now, its face had a nose and a mouth, and the eyes looked more human. Still it was big and ugly and golem-like. Still it was a monster.

"This . . . human female . . . belongs to your brood hive?" Shontill asked bluntly. "I thought . . . Captain

Northern . . . that you preferred . . . meatier specimens . . . with more intelligence.''

"Hey! Listen, muck face," Laura cried, joyfully angry at last. "I don't belong to this guy, and I want to tell you that if I had a blaster you'd be eel bait now! I've caught prettier things fishing in swamps!"

"Captain Northern," said Shontill, with a steady bass throb, "should this . . . bothersome human female . . . prove unsatisfactory . . . to your needs . . . biological or otherwise . . . and you wish . . . of her to dispose . . . may I have . . . the exquisite pleasure . . . of rendering her . . . manure for my . . . horticultural projects?"

"If you think your plants can take it, Shontill. Now be a sport. Your sleep cycle was almost over, and Dr. Mish does want to speak with you."

With a grunt and an evil glare toward Laura, the alien lumbered off, tracking a slimy liquid behind it.

"Tsk, tsk," said Northern. "Poor Shontill is a bother to our clean-up crew after his sleep cycles." He turned and faced Laura. "Now, as to you—"

"You were watching me," she said. "Watching me all the time!"

"Well, of course! Do you expect us to leave you, a Feddy agent, loose without some kind of precautionary surveillance? And now that you've proved your untrustworthiness, you will be confined, under guard, to your cabin until we reach our destination tomorrow."

She fixed him with barely controlled fury. "Wait a moment. If you were watching me . . . you knew what was in store for me inside this room. You knew I might have been—"

"You weren't, were you?" Captain Northern grinned. "Besides, Shontill's troll image is such an act. Inside, he's a pussycat." Northern laughed. "A hungry pussycat sometimes, true, and as vicious as alien pussycats come, but all in all a pussycat."

"I've never seen anything like . . . What planet does he come from?"

"Someplace far away, dear girl, and since you have shown yourself to be totally unreliable, why should I, clearly a remarkably canny individual, trust you with one of the biggest secrets of the *Starbow*? Hmmm?''

"It was . . . you who watched me,'' Laura said, calmer now, considering. "Surely a captain of a large starship has more important things to do.''

"You know, you are perfectly correct,'' said Captain Tars Northern, striding up to her, hands at his sides. "But then, leisure time is so important to one's sanity, is it not?''

He snapped his fingers. Three robots walked in and surrounded Laura Shemzak.

"Take her to her quarters and make sure she does not leave,'' he ordered. "Oh, and, Laura, can I give you a very important bit of advice?''

"What?'' she asked sullenly.

"You might think about growing your hair a little longer. You'd look a little more presentable that way.''

On her way out, Laura Shemzak used a word that Tars Northern was surprised to learn she knew.

It made him laugh, but only after a long pause.

Chapter Thirteen

CAL Shemzak stood somewhere in a maze.

"All in all," he said, sitting down to rest, "I think I'd rather be in New Philadelphia."

The maze did not respond. Nor did the Jaxdron he knew were listening.

He lifted his head from between his knees.

"That's a goddamned joke, guys! I read it in some twentieth-century book. Can I hear some applause for my efforts? Would you at least acknowledge my existence?"

Cal Shemzak realized he was screaming at the top of his lungs. His throat hurt from all this senseless screaming at the aliens. He decided he should stop for a while.

"I've been in this stupid maze for hours now. Do I get fed, or is food what I'm supposed to find? Is that the game, guys?"

He'd woken up inside this crisscrossed, twisting affair of corridors after what had felt like a long sleep. Time was immaterial here . . . even more so than usual, Cal thought, chuckling to himself at the odd interplay of reality and concept.

A bright red arrow had pulsed before him. He had followed it because he'd nothing better to do. At certain intersections of halls in this maze were games of various complexities. The deal was, Cal Shemzak soon realized, that if you figured out how to play the game and then you won the game, a door would open. Whether or not these doors led anywhere special was yet to be seen; Cal had mastered the games and taken the passages, and still he was lost in the maze.

"You jerks won't even feed me, huh?" he muttered crossly. "I work my butt and my brain off for you, and you don't take the time even to dish out some of that awful nutrient slop you've been giving me."

That's what the Jaxdron who'd visited him in his cell had been doing: delivering his dinner.

A roil of protoplasm, a shake of pseudopod, a lowering of slop dish, and then the thing was gone.

Or anyway, Cal Shemzak assumed that the deliverer of the food (which tasted like gravy-covered oatmeal) was a Jaxdron. Ugly fellow. The problem with that assumption was that it might not be true. The Jaxdron might have hired help.

"I gotta tell you guys, this is the worst diet I've ever been on!" He picked himself up and trudged onward.

Around the next section, on the wall next to the outline of a closed door, was a screen with symbols on it. Two sets of parallel lines, intersecting: X's and O's.

"My God, I just don't believe it," said Cal Shemzak. "You guys want me to play tictactoe. You want a genius in quantum mechanics to duke it out with a child's game. Well, just stuff it, okay? I'm going to."

Around the next bend was a table and a chair. Upon the table was a bowl of food with a spoon sticking out.

"You guys have got a sense of humor," Cal Shemzak said, sitting down to his dinner. "A weird one, maybe, but a definite sense of humor.

For some reason, the nutrient slop tasted great.

Chapter Fourteen

THE Milky Way galaxy is a magnificent spiral. A hypothetical viewer placed light-years above its elliptical plane would note trails of trillions of stars, sparkling arms swirling out from the incandescent hub. Throughout this spectacular firework of the universe, which moves in a counter-clockwise fashion, lie nebulae and clusters, sparks shedding off the arms, and the whole is suffused with a glow of spectral softness.

The Second Earth Empire, a.k.a. the Federated Empire, a.k.a. the Federation, occupied a very small section of space in comparison to the Milky Way galaxy. Nonetheless, it held dominion over a thousand occupied worlds. The Free Worlds comprised perhaps three hundred planets; the number changed constantly, because of their relationship to the Federation and the encroaching Jaxdron. Most of these worlds lay far from the core of Federation space, thus making the best use of distance, much as the American colonies did in revolting against Great Britain.

One of the key strongholds on the home spiral arm was Shortchild, a military and factory world. Its primary, Capella, was a Class G yellow sun, quite similar to Sol. Shortchild was suitable for military purposes not only because of its position, but because of its density and mass, 1.12 Earth standard, supplying a heavy concentration of metals vital for the construction of both fortifications and starships.

Because of its defensive importance, Shortchild was heavily defended. A large Federation fleet patrolled the sun's seven planets. Recently the sophisticated Sheffield synchronous satellite defense shield had been placed around Shortchild itself.

The Capellan system was not a hospitable area for pimercs, to say the least, but this was where the *Starbow* was headed.

Captain Tars Northern and Navigator Dansen Jitt were at the helm when the *Starbow* broke out of Underspace, far enough beyond the Capellan planetary system to prevent interference from mass distortion and to elude Federation sensor sweeps.

Laura Shemzak sensed the transition, and so was not surprised when the guardian robots—whom she had gotten to know reasonably well by now—opened her cabin door and bade her follow to the dining hall.

"Mealtimes have a ritualistic quality here, don't they?" Laura said casually to Napoleon Bonaparte. "Three per ship's day, attendance mandatory for all crew at supper . . . Who makes the rules?"

"Why, the captain, of course, mademoiselle," answered Napoleon. "Is this not as it should be?"

"Does the ship belong to him?"

"Belong?" The robot smiled. "Belong to the captain? Ah, that is a difficult question to answer."

"Well, I'm not exactly asking any kind of philosophical head knocker!"

"That statement might easily be debated, mademoiselle."

"And by the way, Nap. What the hell is a mademoiselle, anyway?"

"A robot term. Highly complimentary, mademoiselle."

"Just checking. Can't be too sure about what people are jabbering about here."

Napoleon and the others ushered Laura into the dining hall.

The entire human crew was seated—thirty men and women, at least half of whom Laura did not know.

Laura, who knew that it was not mealtime but who felt perverse and cantankerous enough after her incarceration to exaggerate the coarser aspects of her behavior, glanced down at the table, then looked up. "Where's chow?" she demanded.

"This is a meeting, Laura Shemzak," said Captain Northern solemnly, holding a glass.

"Dammit, if you can drink, why can't I eat?"

Silver Zenyo cast an exasperated glance at the ceiling.

Captain Tars Northern lifted his glass and tinkled ice cubes. "Water, Laura. You know. H_2O. Have some if you like. It's very refreshing, and if you must know, I never drink before an operation in which I am to be personally involved."

Laura seated herself. "So. You can just drop me off and I'll get my blip-ship and come back."

"I wish it were that simple, Laura," said Northern. "If you will remember, we are variously known to the Federation as either pirates or mercenaries. Now, what do you think the Shortchild authorities would do if they found the *Starbow* under their noses?"

"So how do we propose to deliver our young protégée to her destination without endangering ourselves?" a young man whom Laura did not know asked.

Silver Zenyo placed a final buff to her fingernails, then looked up, smiling maliciously. "Why don't we give her a spacesuit and give her a push in the general direction?"

"Is that red polish for those claws, Silver," asked Gemma Naquist, "or have you had a recent kill?"

"Sticks and stones, darling," returned the lacquered beauty.

"Children, bickering is not appropriate here," Captain Northern said, absolutely humorlessly. "Dr. Mish has a few words."

The doctor cleared his voice and set down his always

present sensor board. "Our cloaking device will work up to a certain point. Of course, an orbit around Short-child is out of the question." He chuckled for a moment, then resumed dead seriousness again. "An orbit around the fifth planet will be sufficiently close and safe enough. We can then dispatch one of the shuttlecraft, which I have suitably disguised as an interstellar vessel. Laura Shemzak can be delivered to the capital city, Montezuma, where she will obtain her XT vessel. After that, both ships will rendezvous at the *Starbow*, and we can judiciously retreat to Underspace to decide what the next move will be."

"Fine by me," Laura said. "Just stick me in my blip and I'll be happy as a Venusian clam sucking its pearl."

"Laura, please allow Dr. Mish to finish," said Tars Northern. Something in his tone shocked Laura into silence. He was the essense of authority now, serious as a black hole in a ram scoop.

· "Yes, well, there is one other matter that needs to be discussed, Miss Shemzak," said the doctor. "I am embarked upon a very important scientific project . . . yes, I know that you believe the *Starbow* to be just a pi-merc ship with a rollicking bunch of cutthroats and villains to man it, taking their loot where they can get it. But there is much more here . . . than is immediately apparent. For my project I need a certain quite rare metal."

"Yeah. Attilium," Laura said, regaining her spunk and ignoring the glare from Captain Northern. "That's the transuranic you were rooting round for on the *Zeke*. You said something about the Creature from the Planet X needing it. Extensive dental work?"

Captain Northern sighed, and the doctor's eyes gleamed with good humor.

"Only on the jaws of entropy, actually," the doctor continued. "But yes, that is the element we seek, and as it happens, there is a supply on Shortchild. We'd like to get our hands on some of it, Laura, and we'd like you to help us."

"You will be accompanied by myself and at least two other crew members, Laura," said Captain Northern after a moment of silence. "You will tell the authorities that you were rescued by a mining crew—us—who have brought you to Shortchild. Leave the rest to us."

"And sell out my bosses, huh?" Laura said. "This attilium must be pretty important. Probably gets a good price on the black market. I heard Cal mention it once . . . said he used it in his quantum mechanics experiments. What are you guys trying to do, make a super-bomb to blow up the galaxy or something?"

"For heaven's sake," said Silver Zenyo, "are they substituting sewage treatment plants for breeding vats on Earth?"

"Ours can be a violent life at times," said Captain Northern. "But we do not live for death. Perhaps, Laura, if we learn that we can trust you, you might come to appreciate what we are trying to do here as a group, and as human beings in a troubled time." There was a kindness and a patience in his voice that for some reason infuriated Laura.

"Yeah, sure," she said contemptuously. "Wonderful. I'm so impressed. What do you guys think you are, then, Robin Hoods stealing from the rich, giving to the poor? I've never seen such a sorry military group in my life. If I ever get back to the Federation, you can bet I'm going to tell them not to worry so much about some of the sad-sack pi-mercs cruising around the galaxy like lice. I'm sure that some of the guys in the Navy are going to get a real yuck from the fact that pi-merc brains hide themselves behind dyed flouncy hair or particularly ugly fright masks." She laughed derisively. "But then, most of you haven't got a hell of a lot to hide." She smirked. "And these robots are such—"

Laura was enjoying her speech so much she did not notice Captain Northern's action until it was too late.

The man stood, his face like rock, then leaned across the table and grabbed the top of Laura's jump suit. Hands knotted into fists, he dragged her across the table until her face was only a bare centimeter from his own.

"This is my home," said Captain Tars Northern in a hard but low voice. "And this is my family."

Laura was so surprised she could not move to defend herself before Northern thrust her away from him, hurling her back into her chair. The chair tipped over, sending Laura sprawling on the floor.

"I am captain here, lady," he continued, muscles and veins knotting in his throat. "And I demand respect." His eyes blazed fiercely.

The robots helped the shaken woman back into her chair.

Captain Northern took a drink from his glass. "Now, I and my crew"—he smiled—"and perhaps even the *Starbow* would very much like an apology from that very attractive but very big mouth of yours."

Laura began to smoke inside with fury, but she said nothing.

"My goodness, Silver," said Captain Northern, "and I thought you were the champion pouter of this galaxy."

Laura said, "You know where you can stick your goddamned apology, Northern."

Northern threw the cold water in her face.

With a scream she lunged for him, but the robots grabbed her and held her still.

"In this kind of circumstance, one wishes that the ancient practice of keelhauling were possible in space," Captain Northern said. "No apology forthcoming, Mademoiselle Shemzak?"

"I'd rather burn in hell," she spat, hating him as she had never hated anyone before.

Captain Northern shrugged. "Very well. Then we will accept your nonapology in the spirit with which it was given. Now, Laura, can we get down to business?" The captain turned to the doctor. "Shall we get on with the details?"

He refilled his water glass.

Chapter Fifteen

DR. Mish's plan, supplemented by Dansen Jitt's mathematical computations and Tars Northern's common sense, worked absolutely flawlessly until the party disembarked at the Montezuma spaceport and walked through the sophisticated Security stations. At that point, they met with trouble.

A great deal of trouble.

The robots had done a bang-up job on the shuttle, installing a battered jump-stasis engine as well as worn-out mining equipment that the *Starbow* had scavenged somewhere. Tars Northern, Gemma Naquist, and a robot specifically prepared for the attilium heist stepped into the pinnace along with Laura Shemzak as soon as the *Starbow* had established orbit around Capella's fifth satellite. Because of its smaller bulk, the pinnace was able to use its jump-stasis equipment within the solar system, thus considerably cutting down on a long jaunt, and also masking its point of origin.

As soon as they dropped out of Underspace, the radio blared with demands for their identity. A nearby Epsilon-class skip-cruiser intercepted them, scanned them, and found them acceptable for admission to Shortchild. Captain Northern expertly guided the shuttle down through the planet's atmosphere, slipping through wisps of clouds, whooshing above seas and continents, until they reached a huge city with towering buildings and magnificent highways.

Laura Shemzak watched all of this from her grav-couch, safely webbed in against the G forces. She watched Captain Northern's hands dance over the controls and for the first time realized how beautiful and delicate those hands were. The bastard was a jumbled mass of contradictions. She could not help wondering what those hands would feel like on her skin—and then caught herself, remembering her hurt pride, and how much she wanted to hurt him in return. She hated him, and that felt right and good and normal, because he deserved it, she thought as the shuttle's rocket fire tasted the spaceport's permacrete. She would get even with him someday, she promised herself, and the promise salved the smart of her ego.

"Right, Shemzak," Captain Northern said. He looked bizarre in his space tech's outfit. The others had dressed the part of space miners. Northern had swabbed his face with an ointment that encouraged rapid beard growth, so that now he had a nice stubble. He looked wonderfully grubby. "You're the star of this show. Let's disembark."

A transport vehicle awaited them on the cooling pad.

Their plan was simple enough. Laura would get them passes to the city, then go about her business. The others would then locate the attilium, acquire it, rush back to the shuttle, and return to the *Starbow*. There they would meet with Laura and take off.

Suckers, Laura Shemzak thought as the transport whined to the docking station. I'm gonna get in my blip and just fly. I'll deal with you, Captain Tars Northern, when I return from rescuing my brother.

The Federation soldiers were waiting for them at Security.

"Captain Tars Northern?"

Northern blinked. A dozen guns were aimed at the party. "You must have the wrong man," he said.

"We don't think so, Captain Northern," said the

man behind the helmet. "You and your friends are
under arrest. Laura Shemzak, please step out of the line
of fire. Welcome to Shortchild, Pilot Shemzak. You are
a brave servant of the Federation, and we have suitable
accommodations awaiting you."

Laura laughed. She turned, patted Northern on the
cheek condescendingly, then walked away.

"Laura," Northern said, confusion written all over
his face. "Was this just a ploy to trap me?"

Laura spun on her heel. "I don't do that kind of
thing, Northern. I've told you nothing but the truth. I
haven't the faintest idea why they were expecting you,
and frankly, my dear, I don't give a damn."

"Sure you do," said Northern, a grim smile on his
face as he turned to the Federation commander. "So tell
me, how did you know . . . ?"

"We were told to be prepared should you or your
cohorts arrive with Pilot Shemzak. The orders came
directly from Earth."

"Kat!" said Northern. "My God, Gemma. Kat Mizel
turned us in!"

"Maybe she was pissed because you didn't go back
for her," said Gemma. "Hell hath no fury—"

That was when the robot made its move. "Captain
Northern," it cried, stepping to the fore. "Contingency
Plan C—"

"No!" said Northern.

Energy rifles erupted. Within a moment the robot was
riddled with smoking holes. It collapsed, shuddering.

Soldiers jumped forward and grabbed the humans.
Captain Northern was hustled forward. He did not
resist until he was even with Laura. Then he stopped
with such power and suddenness that the soldiers on
either arm were almost hurled onto the ground.

His eyes were blue, Laura realized as they found her
. . . so blue they were almost black, but blue
nonetheless.

"I apologize, Laura Shemzak, for accusing you of
betraying me," he said. "You are not that way, are
you?"

And he smiled.

Laura shuddered. For the merest moment that dark blue gaze seemed to bore so deep into her that . . .

She looked away. Stuff and nonsense, she thought.

The soldiers resumed their grip on Northern and took him away.

"Farewell, O princess of the starways," Captain Tars Northern called out as though addressing a distant balcony. "I pray you find your fascinating brother and spend the rest of your days in sibling bliss!"

"And I hope you rot on some forsaken prison planet!" Laura called after him, not really knowing why she was so furious.

Northern began to laugh.

Soon he and his companions were swallowed up by the exit.

"Damn him!" Laura murmured.

"I'm sure that a man of Tars Northern's reputation will be dealt with in a suitable fashion."

Laura turned and found herself facing a corpulent man dressed in high Federation garb. He offered her his hand and she reluctantly shook the damp, pudgy thing.

"Allow me to introduce myself," the man said, chin working above a pile of tie, collar, and dewlaps. "I am Charlang Dubo, Governor of Shortchild. Overfriend Zarpfrin directly contacted me concerning your capture by these four renegade pi-mercs. Thus I was ready for their arrival. I count myself fortunate to be of service to yourself, to Overfriend Zarpfrin, and to the Federation."

"Subspace radio quark spurt, huh?" Laura said. "That's damned expensive. Captain Northern must be pretty important."

"I believe that the Overfriend has a personal score to settle with Tars Northern," the smarmy fellow said, beady eyes taking in Laura with great pleasure. "And now, my dear, the Overfriend mentioned a starship named the *Starbow*. My dreadnoughts are poised to pounce upon this vessel, just as soon as you let us know where it is!"

"Yeah," said Laura. "That's Northern's boat all right."

"Then you can direct us there, Pilot? This would be a great service to the Federation. A ship like the *Starbow* is a slippery devil to capture and must be approached on tippy-toes, as it were."

Laura frowned. "You know, Governor, if I knew where that damned thing was, I'd sure as hell tell you. But it just let us off and zapped right back into Underspace." She didn't know quite why she was protecting the *Starbow*, but the self-righteous pig standing beside her had instantly antagonized her.

"But Captain Northern must have designated a rendezvous point!" Dubo said, brow beetling.

"If he did, I don't know what it was. He took me down here, you see, so he could get past your security and pull off some kind of heist. That was the bargain, and that's all I know. So ask him, Governor. Not me."

"Ah. I see. Alas, some torture might be necessary before we could extract that information from Captain Northern."

"Where are you taking him?"

"Central Detention. Quite near the XT Experimental Factory, actually."

"Good. Maybe I'll be able to hear him scream." Laura grinned. "Well, I've wasted enough time. Take me to my blip-ship, Governor. I'm not here for parties."

Chapter Sixteen

LAURA Shemzak was almost beside herself with joy and awe. The blip-ship was a bullet-shaped cylinder, three meters long and two high. Silver-hued and sleek, it shone in the strip lighting.

"It's the most beautiful thing I've ever seen," she said, stepping forward to touch it.

"We *have* redesigned the casing, but not only for aesthetic purposes, Pilot Shemzak," said Engineer Peo Logir, regarding the bright new blip-ship proudly. "Now that the XT models are to be fully maneuverable not only within atmospheres, but on planetary surfaces, there had to be some streamlining done to the hull. And I think you'll be pleased with the other changes in this model as well." He smiled at her kindly. "It's going to be like a second body to you, Laura. A better body."

"Something wrong with the one I've got?" Laura demanded indignantly.

"Absolutely nothing. But I don't think it has quite the . . . ah . . . flexibility and utility of this particular XT."

Laura opened her mouth to comment, but decided to allow the engineer to get on with his lecture. "Gotcha. So tell me more."

"For one thing, the force field power has been

stepped up by a factor of ten," said Logir, scratching his moustache. "And we've remodeled the secondary manual console—"

"Maybe you'd better just show me," said Laura, eager to slip inside her new ship.

"Of course," said the engineer, gesturing for her to follow him. He pulled a packet of papers from his coat pocket as they walked.

"We were sent the specifications of your personalized connection capabilities, and the XT Mark Nine is adjusted accordingly."

"Let's give it a go, then," Laura said, pulling up her right jump suit sleeve as they neared the ship. She tapped the correct sequence of pressure points, then peeled back her skin. She held the exposed mechanism to a plate on the side of the blip-ship. Above her head a circle of multicolored lights blazed on in the ship's side. They pinwheeled for an instant, describing the circumference of a small door.

The hatch opened. A ladder extended itself from the opening.

"Anything different in attachment routine?" Laura asked as she climbed up the rungs.

"Standard, Laura. No reason to change that."

She hoisted herself into the padded cockpit and hit a switch. Vu-screens and panels lit. Lights blinked on, stitching quick sequences on their boards. "Real nice, Logir," Laura said, touching the porous material covering the formchair. "Nothing like the smell inside a new blip-ship."

"It's fully stocked for your journey as well. I think you'll find everything in order, Pilot Shemzak." The engineer looked up at her. "Plug her in, Laura, and see how she runs!" he said eagerly.

Laura de-Velcroed the appropriate flaps on her jump suit's legs, torso, and arms. She untied her scarf and slipped it into a pocket.

She hit a button on one console. Wires fell from the ship's ceiling. More popped onto her lap from the left. Methodically, jack by jack, she began connecting her body and her nervous system to the blip-ship. Finally she took the last jack, and fitted it snugly into the socket at the base of her skull.

"Perfect fit," she shouted down to the engineer. "Ready to switch on power flow."

"Do it!" Engineer Peo Logir said, pleased at the blip-ship pilot's obvious approval.

She hit the proper sequence of toggles on the primary manual consoles. She felt the familiar exhilarating surge as the microcosm of her neurons, nerves, synapses . . . grew. It was almost as though she were a planted seed, extending roots of wire, shoots of metal, branches of power into the universe.

The rush was incredible. Suddenly she saw through the sensors of the XT, felt through the hull. The sense of completion was overwhelming . . . as though she and the ship were one, Alpha and Omega joined, power personified.

She drew her awareness back to body control, looked down at Peo Logir, and said, "Nice. I can feel differences, though."

"You'll like them. Now, if I can bring your attention to an important additional feature in the subsonic articulation of the weapons array—"

"I'm cleared for takeoff?"

"Well, yes, you signed the requisition form in triplicate and defense sensors are alerted to your electromagnetic emanations. But I've got a whole laundry list of the Mark Nine's features that I need to—"

She held out her wire-webbed hand. "So toss up the manual. I'll read it on my coffee break."

Stunned, Peo Logir did as directed.

Laura stuffed the papers safely in a compartment.

"You gonna open the doors, or am I going through the walls?"

"You are in a hurry, aren't you? I'd rather hoped we could have dinner."

"Some other time, sweetheart. I owe you."

The engineer, smiling, disappeared into a little room. Parts of the ceiling slipped back. A wind filled with city

sounds and pollution swept in. Buildings loomed over-
head, breaking up the clear greenish sky.

"Thanks, Peo!" Laura said, broadcasting through
the ship's speakers.

She closed and sealed the hatch, surrendered her consciousness to the blip-ship, fed power to the contragrav
and retro-rockets, and reached for the sky on plumes of
steam and fire.

Fifty meters up, she shifted into hover. She used the
state-of-the-art sensor grid to scan the surroundings.

There it was.

If the blip-ship had a mouth, it would have smiled
mischievously.

In the cell, Gemma Naquist sulked.

"What's your problem?" Northern asked. "You vol-
unteered to go."

"I felt like stretching my legs, okay?" she murmured
in her usual hard monotone. "I didn't realize we were
carrying a Jonah."

"And so now you're grouching in the belly of the
whale." Northern began pacing again, a nervous habit
he'd thought he'd conquered, suddenly resurrected.

"Northern, I've never liked the idea of getting mind-
gutted, and it's particularly galling to know that the
Federation is going to be on the blunt end of the knife."
She shook her head. "When you posted that advertise-
ment on Antares IV, I should have run the other way—
started up a dairy farm, like my parents."

"Gemma, you liked the idea of being a soldier of for-
tune," said Northern, wagging a fatherly finger. "And
you love the life. Now that a bit of misfortune has
rained upon us, all previous choices were wrong?"

Naquist bit her lip and looked away. "Do you think
they'll come and rescue us?"

"Who? The U.S. Cavalry?"

Naquist gave him a perplexed look.

"No," he said. "If we're not back by a certain time,
the instructions are to get the hell out."

"Valorous, dutiful, stupid Captain."

"It's the group that matters, Gemma, you know that. The Cause." He smiled sadly at her. "The Ship."

"Well, if they want to risk their necks, I'd be happy if they came for me!"

"It would be suicide, Naquist. You know that." He sat beside her. "I just had a lovely thought. You know that I've always thought you are quite beautiful. And since we don't know just what's going to become of—"

The wall opposite them dissolved.

Captain Tars Northern took his hand off Gemma Naquist's knee and stood, waving away the smoke. When the dust cleared, he saw the magnificent view provided by their perch forty stories above ground . . . and some kind of ship hovering in the middle of it all.

An alarm began to blare.

"Okay, Northern, listen up, 'cause there's no time to argue," said a low-pitched amplified voice.

"Laura Shemzak!" Gemma Naquist said.

"This is the deal, Northern," said the augmented voice from the ship. "I give you a ride back to your shuttle and help make sure that shuttle gets back to the *Starbow*. You and your crew and the *Starbow* help me liberate Cal from the Jaxdrons."

"That's a terribly difficult task, Laura, that bears a great deal of—"

" 'Bye." The blip-ship started to drift away.

"Wait!" cried Gemma Naquist. "We'll do it!" She turned to Northern. "Or am I going to have to personally kick your ass down there!" She pointed down to the street.

"Outvoted, it seems, Laura," called Northern, cupping his hands. "Deal!"

The blip-ship returned.

"So let us in!" Gemma Naquist said. Already the guards were at the door.

"Who said anything about in?" returned the blip-ship. "You will notice several bars inset on the hull, aft, just a short jump away. Hop on, buccaneers!"

Gemma was aghast.

"Tallyho, my dear," said Northern, recklessly leaping. His hands grasped the bar. He swung his feet over another and locked his knees around it securely.

The door to the cell began to open.

Gemma Naquist cursed and jumped. She caught the bar but one hand slipped. Northern helped her into position as the cell door burst open and a guard stepped in, holding a power pistol.

A stun beam from the blip-ship dropped him.

"Hang on to your heads," said Laura Shemzak, and the blip-ship streaked away toward the spaceport.

"Farewell, cruel world!" cried Captain Tars Northern, hanging on to the bars for dear life.

Gemma Naquist wasn't sure if he was laughing or screaming, and she was too preoccupied to care.

Laura Shemzak was careful with her air speed on the trip back to the shuttle. Her computer continuously calculated the atmospheric conditions and made sensor readings on her passengers to determine the air pressure they could take. She was also careful to leave the automatic peripheral force screen off, since that would instantly kill them in their quite precarious—and very amusing—condition.

With a jaunty confidence, she flew to the shuttle while Captain Tars Northern and Gemma Naquist clung to the hull, the wind whipping their hair and clothes.

Laura kept her vessel low to prevent easy radar detection and swept the radio bands for news of the breakout. It wasn't long in coming: a police bulletin was broadcast. Although the blip-ship and its passengers had not been located, an alert concerning the escaped prisoners was on the air. It was a confused and inaccurate report. Apparently her action had not merely caught the defense team by surprise; it had caught them napping.

When the spaceport came into view, her telescopic viewers indicated that no special guard had been placed around the *Starbow*'s shuttlecraft. As they drew closer, Laura keyed a detailed sensor sweep for signs of human activity.

She slowed down enough to allow her amplified voice to be heard above the screech of the wind.

"Listen up, guys," she said. "I read two security men nosing around the shuttle, equipped with hand weapons, so keep your tails close to Momma."

"We read you, Mom," returned Northern. She heard him clearly through the ship's sensors. "Just don't drop your litter yet. We're still a little high up!"

The blip-ship descended toward the landing pad where the shuttle pointed its nose somewhat less than majestically toward the sky. The two security men were just emerging from the hatch and climbing down the ladder, looking neat and smug in their uniforms, apparently still unalerted as to who might be paying a visit.

One of the men happened to look up and saw the shiny cylindrical vessel coming their way. He turned to call his companion, then lifted a wrist radio. But it was too late. Laura had them within the range of an electronic disruptor beam, and in moments they dropped unconscious to the permacrete.

"Think you can take it from here?" she asked her shaken passengers as she hovered two meters off the pavement.

"Oh, sure," said Naquist. "All in a day's work." She kicked free of the ship and landed on both feet.

"You'll cover for us?" Northern asked before he let go of his set of bars.

"I always go the extra light-year, Captain."

"Thanks," said Northern, and dropped.

Laura stood sentry as the two scampered for the shuttle. When the hatch was closed, Laura established radio contact.

"I think we'd better hurry," she said. "I read a couple of military vehicles zooming our way fast."

"Roger," returned Northern's voice.

The shuttle jumped as its antigrav motors turned on. Within moments it was hovering above the pad.

"Okay," said Laura, as a bit of laser fire touched her just-turned-on deflector shields. "We're out of here!"

• • •

Within minutes the two ships had escaped the planet's atmosphere; the bright, color-streaked globe that was Shortchild fell away from them like a child's toy.

Ahead, however, three points of light were growing in size.

"Jesus," said Northern, strapped beside a control console. "Federation battleships! Three of them. I didn't know I was that important!"

Gemma Naquist's attention was focused on the jump-drive readings. "Come on, you bucket of bolts, move it!"

"How much longer before we get free of significant gravity and key the jump?" Northern asked.

"At this rate, another three goddamned minutes!"

"We're going to have to take evasive action, then. We've got a couple ships on our tail, and part of the fleet meeting us head on."

"We can't. That would treble the time before we can safely jump. Make evasive maneuvers, yes, but keep going in this direction or we'll never get back to the *Starbow*. Thank God we've had time to alert the folks back home about our return."

"Midshipman," chided Captain Northern. "I hope our blippie friend is still riding shotgun."

"I really don't think it's the right time to be calling her names, Captain."

A quick sensor check placed the blip-ship pacing them less than half a kilometer away. Laura was already aware of the Federation ships.

"I'll do my best as a distraction," she said. "I want to check out how much firepower this baby has, anyway."

Within ninety tense seconds, the Federation vessels were within visual range. Two cruisers, one dreadnought, they were all ellipsoids bristling with weapons.

"Begin evasive maneuvers," said Naquist.

"Can't we jump now?"

"Still not in safety zone. We'll be pushing it as it is."

"Damn. This thing really wasn't built for a space battle. I'm putting full power on deflector screens."

Gemma glanced down at the radio needles. "We've got something coming in on Federation band, Captain."

"Put it on. If they're talking, they won't be shooting!"

Naquist obeyed, hands playing expertly over the radio controls. ". . . This is GFS *Churchill* . . . to shuttlecraft . . . we have you within firing range. . . . Notify us of your surrender immediately, or we will proceed with destruction procedure. . . ."

"Tell them we surrender," said Captain Northern.

"What?" Naquist was aghast.

"It'll just buy us time!"

Naquist shook her head and keyed open the transceiver. "Roger, *Churchill*. We read you. Please notify as fo approved method for safe surrender."

The timer revealed fifty-four seconds until safe jump.

As the *Churchill* began to relay the surrender procedures, a voice erupted over another set of speakers.

"Hey! I didn't rescue you to have you surrender!"

It was Laura.

"She must have been listening in. Tell her it was just a ploy!" commanded Northern.

The blip-ship was visible now on the vu-screen.

With astonishing speed it streaked closer, letting loose a beam of power that sizzled through the shuttle's low-power force screens and blasted off a rod of protruding weaponry.

"We're not surrendering, Laura! It was just to buy time!" Gemma Naquist yelled into the transmitter.

"Got it—sorry," Laura's voice came back.

"Back to original plan!" Northern said desperately. "Man the lasers, Naquist. I'll do the evasive maneuvers."

It took the Federation ships only a few seconds to respond to the blip-ship's action. Streams of energy crackled from beamers, converging on Laura Shemzak. But she avoided them easily. She flitted around the ships with incredible agility, firing her own weapons and always scoring.

If he'd had time, Northern would have enjoyed the spectacular display of action and pyrotechnics as the amazing blip-ship danced widdershins around the Federation behemoths; but he had to concentrate on making his course as erratic as possible as it threaded past the enemy ships—without losing his path to a safe jump to Underspace.

"My God," said Naquist. "She's amazing!"

"What's the time?" Northern demanded.

"Eighteen seconds to safe jump, but we have to be clear of these ships!"

"Roger. Just one more zigzag and we'll make a run for it. I—"

Suddenly the shuttle rocked hard. A shiver of light cascaded down the vu-screen. A few circuit boards blew in the walls, filling the cabin with smoke.

"Forget the evasive maneuvering," said Northern. "I'm just making that run!"

His fingers found the appropriate controls.

Since they were now past the Federation ships, Naquist directed the vu-screen to starboard. The picture showed the blip-ship still tirelessly skipping and jumping among the dreadnought and the cruisers like some mad glowworm on speeded-up film.

A sudden spectacular explosion rocked the aft of one of the cruisers. "My God," said Naquist, "that woman has just knocked the hell out of one ship's engines!"

"Wonderful," said Northern grimly. "What's the time?"

"Three seconds to go."

"Let's get out of here!"

Naquist's hands obediently pulled the correct levers. The jump-stasis engine kicked in, and the shuttle rattled insanely as it was ripped from normal space and flung to where its mother ship waited.

Chapter Seventeen

"CAPTAIN Northern," said Dansen Jitt, helping his commander out of the smoking shuttle, "you look terrible."

Tars Northern's hair was singed and tousled, his face gritty. He coughed and squinted at the navigator. "Who's at the helm?"

"Arkm."

"Tell him to get us into Underspace. Now. There are a couple of battleships on our tail—the kind that eat moons for breakfast."

"But the stress on the ship—"

"The *Starbow* is going to have to take that stress," said Northern, "or take about a sun's worth of energy blast from Feddy ships."

Fear clear in his expression, Navigator Jitt raced to the communicator.

Northern turned to watch the robots cooling the shuttle with CO_2 from fire extinguishers. Wiping soot off her face, Gemma Naquist emerged from the hatchway and stepped down the ramp.

"She's not going to blow," she announced. "Next time we go out for a jaunt in a shuttle, though, let's check the wiring, okay? That beam from the Federation cruiser just grazed us, and you would have thought we'd gotten hit by a comet!'' She looked around. ''Laura get in all right?''

''Right on our tail,'' said Northern.

''Which she covered real well,'' said Naquist, shaking her head. ''Tars, she put that cruiser right out of commission. That thing was a thousand kilotons if it was an ounce. What kind of ship is that?''

''A blip-ship,'' said Northern, looking back to where the XT sat in its impromptu berth. ''Catchy name, eh? Rather rolls off the tongue.''

''Well, whatever it is, I want to thank the pilot!'' said Naquist, walking forward to the sleek vessel.

''Our rescue was not exactly performed out of the kindness of the dear lady's heart,'' Northern reminded her.

Naquist turned around and smiled. ''But it does dovetail very nicely with certain intentions. . . .''

Northern raised a thick eyebrow. ''Yes. I think if we get out of this system alive, all will turn out to everyone's benefit.''

The hatch to the blip-ship opened.

Laura Shemzak leaned out, riddled with wires.

''Hair curled yet?'' Captain Northern asked pleasantly. Laura grinned.

One by one, she took the wires out of their jacks and refastened the skin flaps. She then tied her red scarf around her neck. Northern and Naquist were watching this exhibition when the jolt signaling entry into Underspace hit them.

''Faster than I expected,'' the captain said. ''Arkm's a good pilot.''

''You might have told me,'' complained Naquist. ''I like to strap in for stuff like that.''

''Just one more bump on the roller coaster,'' said Laura, climbing down to the floor. ''Can I have a glass of water?''

Naquist looked puzzled for a moment, then went to get one.

''So. Why did you rescue us, Laura?'' Northern asked. ''You were free and clear. Now you're going to have to answer to the Federation for helping a couple of criminals escape, for stealing a blip-ship, and for doing a great deal of damage to Federation merchandise."

Laura smoothed her jump suit, not answering. Gemma returned with the glass of water.

Laura accepted it with quiet thanks, then tossed the water in Tars Northern's face.

"Maybe that's why," she said, stalking away, planning on taking a nap.

Behind her, Captain Tars Northern, dripping, smiled, because he knew it wasn't.

Not the whole reason, anyway.

Selected members of the *Starbow* crew sat in the meeting room, listening as Laura finished up her briefing. A holographic star chart occupied one wall. Laura utilized a light-plotter to illustrate her presentation.

"And so computer analysis indicates that the most likely destination for the Jaxdron ships is the occupied world Baleful." She drew a purple line around the dot representing the planet in the Coridian system. "Marchgild sector, my friends. Not terribly far. Won't take a great deal of time from your busy schedule of raping and pillaging."

That comment, Laura could see, went over like a lead balloon. Blank expressions faced her as the crew considered.

"The Jaxdrons are an unknown quantity," said Dansen Jitt. "Frankly, I don't like this at all."

"No one is asking you," said Captain Northern. Laura was pleased to see that he was in a deadly serious mood. He had followed all of her lecture with rapt attention. "Didn't I make myself plain? The pilot has my pledge. This is not a voting situation, Navigator."

"Well, excuse me for living!" Dansen Jitt said, folding his arms over his chest. "I just wanted to point out that no human vessel has ever entered Jaxdron space and returned!"

"Let's be the very first on our block, okay?" Naquist said. "Go on, Laura. Excuse our token wimp."

Laura nodded. She and Gemma had grown closer since the incident on Shortchild. Laura had the feeling that Naquist not only felt gratitude, but actually liked the blip-ship pilot.

"That's about all I can say right now. I've not studied the data placed in my ship's computer. I thought I'd share that openly with you all, since we're working on this mission together now"—she glanced at Northern—"now that I'm no longer persona non grata."

"That is quite true," said Captain Northern, folding his hands together. "Temporarily, you may consider yourself a member of the crew."

"I'm truly overwhelmed, Captain," Laura said sarcastically.

"And as a crew member, there are some things you should be made cognizant of," Northern continued, brushing back his recently clipped hair. "Aspects of our history, reasons for the consensus reality that we have tried to create among ourselves."

"Well, if you're going to tell me wonderful secrets, Captain, could you use something close to neo-English?" Laura said, hands on hips.

Dr. Mish put down his sensor board. "You forget, my friend, they do not teach philosophy to the Federation *untermensch*."

Laura glanced quizzically at the doctor. These guys were all loony.

"Ah!" Northern said. "All action and adventure for our new crew member." He took a flask from his jacket pocket, opened it, and saluted Laura. "Adventure and hairbreadth escapes." He took a drink.

"Tars," Dr. Mish said in a soft voice.

Northern grinned at the doctor like a little boy caught with his hand in a cookie jar, then stepped over and handed the flask to the man.

"Now then," he said, "to come clean with our guest." He cleared his throat. "It is entirely within our interest to locate your brother as well.

"I'm not saying that we would have given it a shot without your arrival," Northern continued. "But with all your valuable data on the subject, and our reckless natures—"

"I don't understand at all," Laura said. "Something smells fishy here."

"Perhaps it's Shontill, standing right behind you!"

He laughed as Laura jumped.

The alien stood in the doorway, its bulky humanoid form outlined by a hallway light.

"Shontill, don't be shy!" Northern called. "Come on in and join our meeting!"

"Is this some kind of joke?" Laura demanded, backing away. "Keep that thing away from me, Northern!"

Shontill stepped through the holograph, the stars glittering on his bulk. He looked at Laura with an unreadable expression on his face, then went to the table, where he sat by Silver Zenyo.

"For once I can agree with you, Shemzak," Silver said, getting up, nose wrinkled with disgust. She sat down at the other end of the table, smoothing back her new hairstyle.

"I think that our alien guest should be accorded more respect," Northern said, somber again. "He is, after all, important to us all, though in different ways."

"That's news to me!" Laura said.

Northern stood beside Shontill and placed a hand on his shoulder. The alien wore a dark brown robe over his light green body. His skin seemed softer now, his large eyes somehow kinder. Laura noticed a fine coat of dark fur covering his cranium and running down his neck, like a brown crest. The deep green intelligent eyes, unreadable, were focused now on Captain Northern.

"Attilium," said Northern. "Tell us about attilium, Shontill."

The skin flaps over Shontill's nostrils quivered. He opened his mouth and disgorged a barely decipherable rumble. "You promised . . . to bring Dr. Mish . . . and myself . . . attilium. Attilium . . . was on . . . that last planet."

"As you can see, Laura, Shontill is a bit fixated on

the stuff." Northern patted the alien's broad shoulder. "Yes, that's quite true, Shontill. But we had some misfortune, my friend. We didn't get any, and escaped by the skin of our teeth."

"Human teeth . . . have skin?" Shontill said. "A clear mark . . . of genetic . . . inferiority."

"Just a saying, Shontill. Now, Laura here would like to know about attilium."

"Attilium . . . is key . . . to my race!" Shontill announced fervently, his eyes ablaze. "Attilium . . . is my . . . one hope!"

"Dr. Mish, apparently Shontill can't remain dispassionate on the subject long enough to deliver a simple lecture. Would you do the honors?"

"Certainly." The white-haired doctor pondered his wording for a moment, then turned his fine-boned features to Laura. "Attilium is a transuranic, that is, a rare and very heavy metal that contains quite a few more active . . . very active . . . electrons than uranium. And quite a few more fascinating other subatomic particles. As a blip-ship pilot, Laura, I suspect you realize that Underspace was discovered mathematically long before its use was achieved."

Laura nodded.

"Well, there are other forms of mathematics—new forms—that reveal other things about the nature of holistic reality."

"There is more in heaven and earth than is dreamed of in your mathematics, Horatio," Northern commented blithely.

Dr. Mish ignored him. "Just as Underspace might be termed a different dimension from the ones we inhabit normally, so, it is speculated, there may well be other dimensions. The special properties of attilium are such that part of the element, apparently, exists in a special different dimension. It is so special that everyone—the Federation, the Jaxdrons, and yours truly included—would love to discover its secrets. This, we believe, was what your brother Cal was working on. This is why the

Jaxdrons kidnapped him.''

"So why is this new dimension so terrific?" Laura asked.

"Very simple. Theoretically, if it can be pierced and navigated, it will be a faster avenue of interstellar travel than the dimension we call Underspace."

Laura nodded. "I see. In other words, whoever gets it first will have the upper hand—in trade, in war . . . in everything!"

"Exactly."

"So why does Shontill get so hot and heavy on the subject?"

Shontill turned to her. "The Jaxdron . . . destroyed my planet . . . my race. The few survivors . . . escaped to this dimension. I seek them . . . I seek my race. I am . . . the last here. I am . . . lonely."

Northern, face grave, turned to Laura. "We found Shontill, stranded in the wreckage of his starship, near the fringes of the Horsehead Nebula, out on the rim of known space. He was in suspended animation, and had been for perhaps two centuries our time."

"Then there are other intelligent races with stardrives in this galaxy," Laura said unemotionally but with interest.

"It's a very large galaxy, my dear," Dr. Mish replied casually. "But the Frin'ral, Shontill's people, knew of no other—pardon the expression—stardriven race until they encountered the Jaxdron."

"Generally a malevolent bunch," Northern noted drolly. "As you might infer from the evidence presented, to get on with the exposition, we would all like to gain access to this dimension—Omega space, Dr. Mish has dubbed it—for our own particular reasons."

"I understand the Federation reasons . . . and I can certainly understand why the Jaxdron wanted my brother now. Shontill's story makes sense. But what's in it for you, Northern, hmmm? What's in it for you and the *Starbow* and its crew? Discover the secret, then sell it to the highest bidder?"

Northern smiled mysteriously. "Perhaps, Laura. But

then, this goes beyond what you need to know. Suffice it to say that our commitment links handily to yours. Serendipity in action, eh?"

"Yeah, thrilled, I'm sure."

Northern said, "Mr. Jitt, will you please make the necessary adjustments to plot the course to Baleful."

"Reluctantly, sir."

"Naturally. And how long do you estimate that this little jaunt will take at maximum speed?"

"Maximum, Captain?" Engineer First Class Elmond said. "Is that necessary?"

"We have promises to keep, Engineer," Northern said. "And parsecs to go before we sleep. Jitt?"

"Approximately six days, sir. But may I say—"

"No, Navigator," he said. "Ours is not to reason why."

Laura walked up to Shontill. "Well, as long as we're going to be crewmates, we might as well bury the hatchet. I'm sorry I barged in on your nap the other day." She held a hand out to shake.

Shontill looked at it with what could only be described as a blank expression. Suddenly he took the hand and popped it into his mouth.

Laura withdrew her hand, looking with horror at the yellowish slime that now coated it.

"What the hell was that supposed to be?" she cried. "A tasting?"

"Is this not . . . a form of . . . greeting among . . . your race?" Shontill said.

"No, you idiot. You shake hands, or paws, or tentacles or whatever it is you've got!"

"A definitely . . . intriguing tingle . . . on the sensory nodes," Shontill said, as Laura found a napkin to wipe her hand.

Northern raised an eyebrow. "I don't think it would be wise to get accustomed to that taste, Shontill." He looked over to Laura. "Well, my dear lady, I must say that I am most intrigued at the notion of examining your blip-ship's interior."

"Tell you what, Northern," Laura said, still eyeing

Shontill suspiciously. "You show me yours, I'll show you mine."

"Within prescribed limits on both our parts, Laura Shemzak," said Northern. "And by all means let's beware of intriguing tingles!"

Chapter Eighteen

GAMES, games, games, thought Cal Shemzak. What do they think I am, a chimpanzee?

He flung away the latest intricately layered, multi-colored puzzle. Its hard and soft plastic pieces clattered and bounced against the wall.

"So give me a banana, then!" he cried hoarsely, tears starting from his eyes. He slumped against a wall, hands over his unshaven face. "Give me something other than that goddamned slop you've been rewarding me with!"

Bleary eyes looked out hopefully from between his fingers. God, he felt grubby. Grubby and rotten. "And how about a nice bath, too!" he murmured.

The last bowl of slop had not agreed with him. Perhaps that was why he had done so poorly on his last puzzle-test, precipitating his tantrum.

Cal Shemzak had no idea how many days or nights he'd been on the Jaxdron ship. Without any kind of chronometer, time was meaningless, a mere concept, measurable only in the length of his beard or his fingernails.

They had taken him out of the maze a while back and placed him in a domed chamber with featureless walls, which would occasionally flash with odd conglomerations of color. From time to time a puzzle or a game of some sort would emerge from a hole in the wall. Cal's duty was clear: he had to solve the puzzle or figure out and play the game. Then he would place it back in the hole, a sliding door would close, and when it opened again, a certain portion of nutrient slop would lie in its place as a reward for his industry.

It rather reminded him of education in Lifeschool back home, all very meticulous and calculated toward some inscrutable end. Learn this, absorb that, become the machine our tests show you can be! Show how superior you are to your fellow students, achieve, serve the Collective Good! Learn to connive and manipulate for the scraps of power we throw you to feed the very hunger we have created in you! Cal Shemzak had always considered himself smarter than his teachers. After all, hadn't he had the brilliance and daring to use his computer to break into all kinds of fascinating things? Hadn't he flaunted his rebelliousness under their noses time after time, sneaking out of Bunker, exploring the dusty archives of yesteryear below City? Hadn't he shown his contempt for the System by creating a relationship, with Laura, that was contrary to the line he had to toe?

A brief flicker of pride, self-satisfaction, of genuine love for Laura, gave way to a looming question.

If he'd been such a rebel, such a danger, why had they allowed it? Surely, with their machines, they knew something of Cal Shemzak's antics. Yet though he and Laura insisted upon sharing a last name as a token of their sibling state, Authority did nothing to prevent the two from seeing each other.

The question gave way to a revelation: Because they didn't really care. If Cal's rebellion had been a real threat, they would have slammed down their fist so fast . . . and then just scooped his re-formed gray matter back into his skull the way they wanted it. That's why the System worked so well, had lasted so long; while monitoring everything, channeling its components toward its own ends, it allowed people a little slack. That was enough to create an illusion of independence, of individuality, to satisfy the craving for freedom. The Authority capitalized on both the good and the bad in human beings for its own mindless, mechanical purposes.

And the worst of it, Cal now knew with every fiber of his exhausted being, was that the Federation existed not because it was good or bad but because it worked. And the reason for its existence was to continue working . . . to survive . . . to carry on its machinations . . . to spread its machinery like webbing from star to star. . . .

Cal suddenly realized he was lying on the floor, doubled up. The room seemed to be closing in on him, then ballooning out. Colors throbbed, skewed, ran in rainbows across the floor to vortex into a maelstrom of meaninglessness, and Cal knew that there must have been something weird in that food because music suddenly boomed soft in his pulsing head and a . . .

DARKNESS

. . . opened up to another room.

Cal was lying upon his back. He got up, and was immediately aware that he felt better. In fact, he felt great. He wore a freshly washed pair of coveralls. He could no longer smell his own body odor. His hair was cut, and his beard shaven.

The new room was smaller and less well lit, but otherwise as featureless as the other room, except for a door, which was slowly opening.

"Hello?" Cal said.

An alien stepped into the room. It was about four feet tall, with five eye stalks squiggling above a wartlike protrusion between its shoulders. It wore a robe and carried a rod, which crackled with electricity at one end.

Cal held up his hand as a sign of peacefulness.

The rod blazed. A beam ripped through the air, and before Cal could even feel the pain, his hand was just smoking ash. A bare bone rose up out of cauterized skin.

Cal screamed. Instinctively he turned and ran.

With a crackle, the energy beam blazed again. Cal was aware of an impact, a pressure on his back.

Abruptly the ray blazed ahead of him, emerging from his chest.

Cal Shemzak froze, noted the blackened hole, the gaping ribs, and realized that he was dead, and before the pain could arrive there was . . .

DARKNESS

. . . which seamlessly raised its curtain to the sounds of some sort of animal in nearby trees.

The air had a strange sweetness to it, an alien tang. The sky was softly bright, with scatterings of pale pink clouds and a mountainous horizon. Wind-stirred water slapped the sides of a permacrete swimming pool. The air tasted of chlorine.

Cal lay on a deck chair, beneath an umbrella. He looked at his right hand, which was intact, and then down at his chest, which was fine, covered by a silken robe.

He felt immensely peaceful, as though he had just awakened from a long, reviving sleep.

Ice cubes tinkled as a tray was placed on a glass table beside him.

"Gin and tonic, sir," said the butler.

"Where . . . where am I?" Cal demanded.

"An atmosphere dome on a planet called Baleful, Mr. Shemzak," said the man, straightening his tie. He was perhaps fifty, and wore a uniform—a suit with tails, and a raised collar, neo-Edwardian style.

"Are you a Jaxdron?" Cal demanded.

"Goodness no, sir. Merely a colonial in the service of the present Masters of this world. My orders are to see that you are kept comfortable until things are prepared."

"Things? What things?" Cal looked around. Behind him was a large, beautiful house. "What is going on here? What do they want from me?"

"May I advise you, sir, that I have learned that, when dealing with the Jaxdron, questions of why are quite ill advised, because the answers, when received, are more confusing than the original condition in which the questions were conceived."

"I'm beginning to get that impression as well," Cal Shemzak said. "Baleful, you say. Right on the Underspace fault . . . dead-center mathematical correspondence!"

"If you say so, sir."

"So that's why they wanted me," Cal said, picking up and sipping his drink. It was startlingly good, crisp, chill, with a limey tartness. "When do I get to meet my new employers?" Cal asked.

"That is difficult to say, sir," replied the butler. "I am not entirely sure I have actually met them myself."

"You're a great help . . . whoever you are."

"Wilkins, sir. At your service." The butler bowed.

"Damn," Cal said. "If I'm so close to Federation space . . ." He looked at the butler. "I have a sister."

He looked up at the pseudo-sky.

"She's going to try and rescue me." Cal Shemzak was not sure whether to be pleased, worried, or distraught at the notion.

"I believe, sir, that that is what the Jaxdron are counting on," Wilkins said. "Dinner is at six, sir. I think you'll be pleased with Cook's menu."

Chapter Nineteen

MANKIND dreamed of Underspace long before mathematicians and physicists declared, through computation, its probable existence. It took some time to develop the technology to enter the noncausal time/space fabric and learn to traverse its strangeness. But it was physicists like Cal Shemzak who were truly coming to understand the implications of the fact that Underspace existed only when it was used to travel the starways, a clearly proven case of viewer-participation quantum physics which, at heart, went against everything Albert Einstein and Sir Isaac Newton stood for.

Laura Shemzak did not understand the principles at all. She was simply an intuitively brilliant pilot, as she was happy to explain to anybody who cared to listen.

"They taught me just about everything there is to know about flying one of their boats," she said, standing with Captain Tars Northern by the docking berth, arms folded, leaning jauntily against a railing, and chewing on a stick of moodgum. "They fooled around with my body so they could connect me up right. But that's not what makes a pilot, is it?"

Northern did not speak, letting a nod suffice.

For a brief moment, Laura felt a strange bond with the man. Somehow he knew what she was talking about,

112

in the way no one but other blip-ship pilots could. How did this jerk know, she wondered, but then she was distracted.

"Hey!" she screamed at one of the robots. "Colonel Blimp! You missed a spot. I want this ship spotless, you hear me?"

"Please," said the robot, hanging in its harness, dripping soapy water from its squeegee and its bucket. "The name is Kitchener. General Kitchener."

"Well, right now you're General Janitor in my book, so do a good job," Laura instructed. "Dr. Mish made this guy, huh?"

"Yes. So you were telling me that there are new features to this XT Mark Nine?" Captain Northern commented.

"Oh, hell yeah! The engineer didn't even have the chance to tell me all of them. I've got the manual in there somewhere. I guess I should take a look tonight, shouldn't I?" Actually, after escaping Shortchild, she had practically memorized the documentation Logir had provided; she just liked to appear casual to show off.

"Yes. Anything will be of definite value when dealing with the Jaxdrons on Baleful," Northern said with a sigh. "It's not exactly going to be a milk run."

"The real value of these babies, I guess," said Laura, examining her ship with pride and wonder, "is that they're so damned maneuverable, anywhere. They can skim right on down into atmospheres just like airplanes, pretty as you please, or function like the most advanced Federation starships in space, or travel on land or even underwater."

"What kind of armament do you have?" Northern asked.

"Standard blip-ship. Lasers, a proton zap, plus a force screen that's supposed to be a real killer in this model."

"Cloaking device?"

"Do Devonian fish-men pee in the H_2O?"

Northern smiled at that. "Can I have a look inside?"

"Sure, just don't touch anything."

Northern climbed the ladder and peered into the tiny cabin. "Nice. I don't suppose Dr. Mish could have a look at all this, could he?"

"Federation wouldn't like that at all," Laura said. "But I suppose I could say you tied me up."

"No. Brainwash. Which might just get you off the hook in regard to your bit of derring-do on Shortchild."

"What makes you think I'm going back, Captain?"

"Come now. You're a Feddy through and through. What's that old saying about the leopard changing its spots?"

"And what do you suppose I'm doing now, Captain Northern?" she asked, annoyed.

"A brief whitewash?"

"And what about you, Northern? Naquist tells me you used to be Federation, too, and so did the *Starbow*, until you and Dr. Mish stole it."

Northern's face hardened, his slightly sunken eyes turned inward. "That is not a subject that bears discussion, Pilot."

"We can discuss me and the Federation. Why not you and the Federation?"

"You know they want my hide for tanning, don't you?"

"I got that distinct impression on Shortchild. Overfriend Zarpfrin seems to have rather a bug up his ass about you."

"Zarpfrin. Yes, of course, this would be his jurisdiction, and he would have the power." He directed at Laura a long, hard look that gave her an uneasy feeling. Then his expression softened, and he let go a laugh. "I'd have loved to see his face when Kat told him what ship she was from, who her captain was!"

"You care to fill me in on the joke?"

"Sure. Why not? Zarpfrin used to be my boss. When Mish and I . . . turned bad"—Northern seemed to savor the words—"he was left holding the bag."

"So why did you do it?"

"Steal the *Starbow*? Become a pi-merc? Maybe we

were bored. Maybe we decided that the Federation was just too confining in its attitudes.''

"There's a hell of a lot more than that, Northern, which for some reason you don't want to tell me."

"And how do you know that?"

"Same way I know how to fly that ship there," Laura said. "From my gut."

"You seem to fit quite a bit in that narrow waist of yours."

"Looks to me like there's plenty of room for what you've got in that swelled head of yours. So how come you won't let some of it go? My brother always told me I was a good listener."

"No, no. That's not a part of our bargain, is it, Laura? I'm just supposed to lend you help and support in your efforts to locate your brother. There was nothing about spilling one's past sins in your lap."

"Sins?"

"A few, here and there, hither and yon," Northern said distantly. "But I've a ship to show you, haven't I?" he said, cheerfully. "And perhaps there are things I can tell you about, Pilot Shemzak. Interested?"

"Captain Northern, I'm all ears."

The *Starbow* seemed a hive of activity: robots worked on shuttlecraft, repaired weapons, did any number of odd jobs; crew members hurried from one room or level to another, with barely a salute for their captain. Northern explained that he had ordered a complete maintenance check of the starship. If she was going into Jaxdron space, the *Starbow* had to be in top shape from stem to stern.

Beyond certain cosmetic differences, the interior of the *Starbow* was fitted quite like any large Federation military starship, which was appropriate, since it used to be one. However, Northern spoke of it in such glowing terms, showing Laura this modification to the Underspace drive engines, or that innovation in the null-grav capabilities, that it was clear the man had a fixation even greater than a ship's captain usually develops. Indeed, Northern spoke of everything as though he had personally placed every single rivet and grommet, as though the *Starbow* were his child . . . or, in a peculiar way, his father.

Although the ship was every bit the technological wonderland, from biochip components to sleek neo-Tao design, Laura could not quite understand the captain's obvious affinity with this one particular vessel. After all, though she was a pilot as well, she approached blip-ships like clothing, or perhaps armor or a second skin, unique and usable, but sheddable and interchangeable. But when Northern ran his hand along a railing, or showed her an interesting design in the furniture, it was as though he were doing some kind of strange striptease, revealing private things about himself.

When she asked about the pods radiating out from the fuselage of the *Starbow,* Captain Northern replied that only certain members of the crew had access to those parts of the ship.

Laura, in a curiously generous mood even though her curiosity was piqued, replied that she understood: her relationship with the Federation not quite certain, she shouldn't know anything that might hurt the *Starbow* eventually.

They had coffee in the mess, and their conversation assumed a quieter, more relaxed tone. Northern asked her about her experience with the Federation, about what she did for it, if she'd ever participated in any battles with the Jaxdron.

The most curious aspect of the vast interstellar conflict that was the Human-Jaxdron war, waged now for almost five years, was how few battles had been fought. The Free Worlds, after all, were principally interested in their own defense. Some had mutual protection treaties with the Federation. Most Free Worlds considered this tantamount to foxes guarding hen houses, but thus far the Federation had been true to the agreements, confirming its fear of the Jaxdron.

The aliens had taken over perhaps ten worlds, all in their own spiral arm, not yet even venturing across the gulf. They seemed to be poking and prodding the bulbous mass of Free Worlds and Federation, testing before taking any kind of big bite. The Federation officially claimed that this maneuvering was because of the sound thrashing Admiral Tarkenton and his fleet had given to a Jaxdron armada in the second year of the war in the Aleph sector, but Laura knew that since only two or three Jaxdron whip-ships had actually been destroyed, this was more propaganda than anything else.

Because of this lack of direct confrontation, Laura had never participated in any move or defense against the Jaxdron. Her function, besides test piloting, had been intelligence work among the Free Worlds with some peace-keeping (and head-banging) on potentially rebellious Federation-held planets. This was the first venture of a blip-ship and its pilot into Jaxdron space.

How ironic, she mused, that a pi-merc vessel should serve as transport!

Northern's attitude toward the Jaxdron seemed nebulous, as though he had no real feelings about the war and would not until he and his starship were actually threatened. Beyond his clear love for his ship and his crew, his loyalties were mysterious. When Laura attempted to delve into his past, Northern diverted the conversation, discussing the merits or history of this or that crew member, not himself.

The crew of the *Starbow* had apparently been recruited in a strange, disorderly fashion. The *Starbow* had plied the Free World backwaters, lighting here and there, lugging cargo, hiring itself out as a mercenary ship, or, eventually, preying on Federation trade vessels and selling the ill-gotten goods to the many black markets that existed in non-Federation space.

During this time, Northern and Mish often encountered individuals with merit who might be suitable for the *Starbow*, but the ones they actually invited aboard had to have one very special quality.

"Desperation," Northern explained to the blip-ship pilot as he poured himself another cup of genuine coffee and added artificial cream and a touch of glucose. "That's what they've got to have. They've got to want something so badly, they're willing to commit themselves, body and soul, not to me necessarily, but to the *Starbow*, and whatever the *Starbow* is involved with, be it raiding a Federation vessel or taking shore leave on some rec planet. Each of their situations is not dissimilar to yours. Oh, of course, there are a few like Dansen Jitt who are desperate in the sense that the *Starbow* is their last chance. But mostly each of the crew members wants something very badly and cannot get it without help. Fornoran Kax, the hydroponics technician, for example . . . a gentle, kind fellow . . . saw his parents killed by a group of raiders on a Betelgeuse planet named New Washington. No one else cared how much he wanted vengeance. We needed him, and he needed us. Last year we found out who those pirates were, and we ran into them at a trading post. We kidnapped their captain and left Kax alone with him and various unsavory torture devices."

Laura had met Fornoran Kax and was shocked. "Kax? Did he kill the guy?"

Northern took a thoughtful sip of his coffee. "No. Didn't touch him. Didn't split a hair. But the captain was pretty shaken at the end of it all, I'll tell you. We let him go." Northern shrugged. "Kax seemed pleased at the outcome and at the end of his commitment time signed on again." Northern smiled. "Says this is his home now, and claims to be very attached to his plants."

"It sounds to me as though another important quality of crew members is general weirdness."

"It doesn't hurt, believe me," Northern answered, assaying her with an unreadable look to his eye. "Welcome to the club . . . for the time being."

"Do I have to sign my name in blood anywhere?" Laura asked with an ironic tone.

"Perhaps you already have," Captain Northern murmured. "But finish your coffee," he said brightly. "Dr. Mish is waiting for us in his"—Northern paused as though considering just the right word—"playroom."

Dr. Mish's "playroom" proved to be a large compartment, occupied by tables strewn with half-finished contraptions: robot heads, torsos, and limbs and odd weaponry. Dr. Mish, looking like a toy maker from some fairy tale, was fiddling with something on a workbench. He barely noticed his visitors until Captain Northern called out his name.

The doctor did not start, but casually turned their way, raising a set of multilensed goggles from his eyes. His shock of white hair was wild and uncombed.

"So this is where the robots get made," Laura said. "I don't suppose there are any little elf helpers tripping about here and there, Doctor."

"You'd be surprised," Northern said.

"Ah. Pilot Shemzak," said the doctor. "I was expecting you, and you are welcome, very welcome. I look forward to examining your XT Mark Nine."

"How did you—"

"Now, I suppose you are probably wondering why you've been allowed to enter this old wizard's sanctum sanctorum. I suppose it's just a matter of fair play. Tit for tat, so to speak. Many secrets in here the Federation would pay a lot of money for." He gestured airily. Then a gleam crept into his eyes. "Do you believe that?"

Laura looked around at the machinery, all meaningless to her. "As a matter of fact, Doctor, the camera implants in my eye are taking detailed pictures for the Overfriends even as we speak."

"Even as we speak!" The doctor clapped his hands together approvingly. "Now then, to business. I understand that even you are not aware of the total capabilities of the new model XT. You mentioned a manual earlier." Laura nodded, accepting that he had been listening to at least part of her conversation with the captain.

"Well, Pilot, I should like to make a simple request. In order to fully orchestrate our rescue attempt for your brother, we're going to need to have a discussion of both your capabilities and ours. I'd like to do that as early as possible tomorrow morning, so I have to ask you to devote your time tonight to that manual, even if you lose sleep over it."

Laura wished she hadn't lied to Northern about the manual.

"Doctor, I should warn you. She flies from her gut!" said the captain, teasing.

"Goddammit, Northern!" Laura said, spinning on him. "Shut your big mouth." She turned back to Dr. Mish. "Of course I will, Doctor. You've already been working with the transfer of relevant information from my ship's computer?"

"Yes, I have. Our auxiliary computer has provided us with a number of interesting possibilities, given our present knowledge of the Jaxdrons and Baleful. I did want to ask you if your brother has any implants like yours. If so, he might well emit some sort of tracking signal we might home in on for identification purposes."

"No. No, not that I know of. Cal was always very proud of the fact that he had no implants. Called himself virgin. Pure as the driven snow. He is a rarity in the age where scientists routinely insert brain augmenter cartridges."

"He hypothesizes from his gut?" asked Northern.

Laura kicked him. "I told you to shut up, Captain!" She turned back to Mish.

"As I was saying, Doctor, Cal wasn't that type, and he was very upset when the aptitude folks came and told me that I was blip-ship material." She smiled wistfully. "He even tried to break into the computer and change my designation, which infuriated me. I wanted to be a pilot, and if I had to carry around some silicon and metal inside me, well, those were the breaks. If that's what they wanted me to do, then fine, I told him. This time, I was going with the flow, and he wasn't, which was strange. I think that's been a problem between us ever since—his inability to accept that even though I've got all this extra baggage, I'm still me. I don't know, Doctor—he has this contempt for things men make, I guess, make and then worship. That's the way he puts it, anyway.''

Dr. Mish nodded thoughtfully. "Yes. Though he seems not to have minded working at the chores the Federation wanted him to.''

"Not exactly. Oh, he'd do the stuff, but he had this incredibly perverse attitude about it, as though it were all just a big sandbox for him and he'd dig the holes they wanted, but he'd also build castles just to knock them over. And they're wonderful castles, and I'm not sure if the Federation truly appreciates them. I know I don't.''

"Castles,'' Dr. Mish said. "An interesting way of terming it. And knocking them over is very important. I look forward to meeting your brother, perhaps even working with him. But I wish your brother's stance on implants had not been so hard. Even a neocortex augmenter would have been useful for detection purposes. We'll just have to risk a quick survey over Baleful before we go in.''

"Wait a moment, Doctor. It just occurs to me. Since we're pretty certain he is on Baleful . . . and if *he* knows he's on Baleful, well, he knows me pretty damned well, and he knows I would try to come for him.''

"You think he'd try to set up some kind of beacon for us?'' Dr. Mish said hopefully.

"I know so!'' She smiled. "And I think I know what sort it might be!''

"My word,'' Northern said, noting Laura's uncharacteristic smile, "I believe we've a beaming brother and sister act.''

He stepped back to avoid any kicks.

Chapter Twenty

WHEN Chivon Lasster was summoned to Overfriend Zarpfrin's office she knew the reason. Lieutenant Kat Mizel of the pirate/mercenary starship *Starbow* had been shipped in yesterday. Overfriend Zarpfrin wanted Lasster there to discuss strategy, now that Mizel had been cleared through security and deemed safe for an audience.

"Small universe, right, Lasster?" the statuesque woman said ironically when Chivon stepped into the Overfriend's plush office.

"I don't know what you mean," Chivon said, for she had never met Kat Mizel before.

The two women examined each other appraisingly, Mizel a little more frank in her stare.

"What I think Lieutenant Mizel means," Overfriend Zarpfrin said, clearly amused, "is that you have both had experience with a certain traitorous Federation pilot who stole one of our starships and became a menace of the starways."

"It's an experience all right," Mizel said through gritted teeth. She was quite lovely in a hard, sour way, classic proportions combined with a powerful, muscular build. The only softness was in her mouth and her violet eyes, eyes that smoldered now at the mention of Captain

Tars Northern. Chivon knew that look well, from the expression in the eyes to the tenseness of the facial muscles. It was the look of a woman scorned . . . a look that she had seen in mirrors some years back.

But how did Zarpfrin intend to use her?

"It was an unfortunate choice on my part when the *Starbow* was in the project," Chivon said. "But as we have been promised, these things are just ripples on the ocean of ourselves."

"I just can't see you and Northern together," Mizel said, shaking her head. "Never knew he went for ice maidens. Oh well," she said sadly, "his tastes are catholic enough, I suppose. He's probably having a high old time right now with that nymphet who conked me on the *Ezekiel*. You know, I always thought that if something like this happened, that bastard would come and get me. But he didn't."

"You see, Friend Lasster, apparently Lieutenant Mizel and the captain were practicing a variant of the barbaric ritual called 'marriage.' "

Chivon Lasster sat down. A kind of emptiness had opened inside of her that had no name. "How ludicrous," she murmured.

"The developments seem clear enough," said Overfriend Zarpfrin. "Quite a coincidence. Two birds with one stone . . . but from all accounts the stone has turned traitor as well." He picked up the reports. "I trust you've gone over these, Friend Lasster."

"I can't believe it," Mizel said, shaking her head. "Did you drill a hole in that blippie's head, too?"

"Her mission was not my idea," Chivon Lasster said.

"Laura Shemzak is a determined woman," said Zarpfrin, "and a pragmatic one as well. Anything she has done, from departing the *Ezekiel* to rescuing Captain Northern on Shortchild, can easily be interpreted as means to her end: to rescue her brother from the Jaxdron."

"You mean she clobbered me and snuck on board the *Starbow* to save her brother?" Mizel said.

"No. She saw it as a faster way to Shortchild. You

were just an expedient, a convenience. I'm sure there was nothing personal."

"So how come she broke Northern out of jail?"

"Having some personal experience with Laura Shemzak," said Chivon, "I can assure you that Captain Northern paid and is paying a dear price for his liberty. We gave Shemzak no aid in this operation other than the use of a new-model blip-ship. I'm sure she jumped at the opportunity of allies."

"No," Kat Mizel said vehemently. "No, it's more than that. He was tired of me. He wanted a new playmate and now he's got one and that's why she did it. A woman doesn't turn and bite the hand that feeds her unless there's another hand fooling around somewhere else." She turned away. "That bastard. He never loved me." Her eyes glistened with tears.

Zarpfrin cleared his throat. Chivon Lasster expected him to deliver a long lecture upon the stupidities of possessive emotions and how the Way of the Friends would cleanse Lieutenant Mizel of her sullied feelings, would redeem her spirit.

But he did not.

"Yes," he said, "I always thought that Captain Northern was an amazingly handsome and charismatic male. He always had a way with women, didn't he, Friend Lasster?"

"Yes," Chivon said uncomfortably, keeping tight rein on her voice. "However, I'm sure that your records will show that if Tars Northern kept . . . company . . . with a woman, he did not seek sexual satisfaction with any other woman. You remember, Overfriend, that this was considered quite an aberration. Northern established firm bonds with his partners, and this was frowned upon by the social examiners and, if I may say so, yourself."

"Well, of course! Such behavior flagrantly flouts our Free Spirit codes. Individual liberty above all except service of the Federation. The Federation gives us the peace and the power to be free." He turned to Kat Mizel. "But as you are from a world which imprisons itself with its separatism, you would not know that, would you? I see, Lieutenant Mizel, why you feel you were wronged. The scoundrel created a bond with you and then deserted you for another. I know that Laura Shemzak is a sexually vital female, and must admit that I myself was not unattracted to her. Does it bother you, then, that, parsecs away, these unimportant bits of biology may be stroking each other even now, whispering promises of undying devotion as they rut their way toward an ecstasy that Captain Northern may never have been able to obtain with you?"

Kat Mizel's face was getting red.

"I always thought that Captain Northern's vaunted integrity was somehow suspect," Zarpfrin said with undisguised glee. "Yet another crime that can be tacked to the man's list."

"You don't know the half of it," Mizel said bitterly. "I could tell you tales of that man's escapades, his drinking, his viciousness and anger, his cruelty—"

"It sounds as though he is a person who must be brought to justice, Kat Mizel." Zarpfrin leaned back in his padded chair. "Of course you must realize that you also are, in the eyes of the Federation, a criminal. We have some interesting punishments, Lieutenant Mizel. Punishments I need not go into, I'm sure, for our purposes. I will also say that your cooperation after your capture aboard the *Ezekiel* allowed us to apprehend Captain Northern on Shortchild. It is not your fault he escaped. For this reason, I have been granted the authority by the council of Overfriends to entreat further cooperation."

"You're saying that if I help you get Northern again, maybe even help get this wretched Shemzak blippie back, then you won't stick me on some godforsaken hellhole prison planet?"

"That is correct," said Zarpfrin. "What is most important, however, is neither Northern nor Shemzak but the *Starbow*. Naturally, we want to apprehend both your . . . husband and Laura Shemzak once they return from their mission. We will not harm them. We merely wish to . . . let us say, correct some faulty circuitry in their minds. So rest assured that your ex-lover will come to no harm.''

"As far as I'm concerned, you can use him for spare body parts, just as long as he knows that it was me who helped you.''

"No matter. However, please believe me, the *Starbow* is a dangerous ship. It must be destroyed, as its sister ships were destroyed years ago. It is a menace to all humanity.''

Lieutenant Kat Mizel was incredulous. "The *Starbow*? It's just a bunch of metal with a stardrive tacked on and a computer to make sure it doesn't smash into any moons. What do you want to destroy it for?''

"Then Captain Northern never confided in you the true nature of the *Starbow*?'' Chivon Lasster said.

"What's to confide? It's just a dandy, fast, maneuverable ship that Northern said he took a shine to and decided to use in his new pi-merc career.'' Mizel seemed genuinely confused.

"Well, if he didn't tell her, he must not have mentioned this to anyone else on the crew,'' Overfriend Zarpfrin said. "Except Mish, of course.''

"Dr. Mish? That crazy old coot?''

Zarpfrin faced the captive. "I am happy that you intend to cooperate with us. I know how much of a threat the *Starbow* is to the human race because I helped create it. I have sworn to track it down before it can harm all that I have dedicated my life to. It is fortunate that we have crossed paths with the *Starbow* and its crew again. I must have the *Starbow*,'' Zarpfrin said, leaning over toward Kat Mizel. "And you are a trump card in my game.''

But Laura Shemzak, thought Friend Chivon Lasster, is the joker.

Chapter Twenty-one

THE *Starbow* slipped out of the mathematical unreality of Underspace back into classical physics millions of kilometers from the rotational axis of the binary stars known as the Witch's Tits.

Laura was on the bridge at the time. The usual feeling of mental and physical disorientation swept through her like a cold shower after a sauna. This was the time a starship was most vulnerable; the *Starbow* crew, dispersed at their stations, were therefore ready for any defensive measures needed.

Nothing awaited them but the stuff of space and a stunning view of the Coridian system: seven planets in orbit around two dissimilar suns, Hecate and Hades, locked into an infernal dance. The backdrop, stars and stars and stars, more stars, it seemed, than darkness, glittered like some magnificent grotto alive with jewels.

"Amazing," said Dr. Michael Mish, glancing down at his sensor board. "A splendidly clean entry. Ship's integrity stands at a virtual one hundred percent. All Underspace emergences should be so easy."

"Because of the Fault, Doctor?" Captain Northern asked.

"Yes, I suppose so. Things in this system are a bit closer to shift point. I suggest that we take that into account in all our actions."

"Course to Baleful, fifth planet in system, plotted and locked into the pilot computer, Captain," Navigational Officer Dansen Jitt announced. "Standard approach at 6 percent light speed, with Baleful orbit achieved in 25.2 GalFed standard hours. And if I may say so, this place gives me the willies, sir."

"Someone pissing on your grave, eh, Jitt?" the communications officer, Lieutenant Tether Mayz said, looking up from her pulse sequence array.

"Well," said Captain Northern, "let's hope it's not a mass burial, shall we?"

Laura looked up from an intense study of Lieutenant Mayz's board. "I don't see a damned thing, Captain. Let me go and scout. I can be there and back in two hours."

"That was not our agreement, Laura," the captain said.

"What the hell do you care, Northern? If I get wasted, then your obligation is through. You can turn tail and run, just like you did to your beloved wife back by the *Ezekiel*!" She placed her hand impudently on her hip.

A brief twinge passed over Captain Northern's face. He swiveled his chair so that he faced away from her. His voice was cool. "Pilot Shemzak, you may not realize that, in our contract, the stipulation was that my duties to the *Starbow* overrode my duties to Lieutenant Kat Mizel."

"You didn't sound real unhappy about my leaving her back in that linen closet!" she said, hoping his anger would prod him into allowing her to jump ahead to Baleful.

"My relieved state was incidental. I am a man of my word, as I have indicated. True, I enjoy the odd dance and debauch within the confines of my agreements, enjoy the occasional joke. Sometimes I exceed the bounds of the polite. However, in the complex weave of my commitments, I have my priorities, and the success of this mission, as well as the safety of my ship and crew, is much more important than a silly little girl's antsy pants!"

"Silly little girl!" Laura said, angry now herself. "Northern, in my four years with the Federation, I have seen things and done things that have put me parsecs away from my silly-little-girl days."

"Gentlemen," said Northern. "Please proceed as ordered—"

"Captain, may I talk to you privately?" Laura Shemzak requested tersely.

"I don't see why not, Pilot. We have plenty of time before we reach orbit around Baleful and our plan proceeds." He turn to First Mate Thur. "Arkm, you have the conn."

In his cabin, Captain Northern went first to the bar, then changed his mind, going to the refrigerator instead for a bottle of seltzer and a lime.

"Back in the old days, sailing ships on Earth, it was the English who discovered that it was their salt pork diet that gave them scurvy and that by carrying plenty of these"—he tossed the green fruit up, caught it—"and eating them, one could get the necessary vitamin C. So though others called them 'Limeys,' the other navvies soon began eating citrus as well." He got out glasses. "Would you care for a drink, Pilot Shemzak?"

"No. I want to know why you won't give me permission to make a simple scouting mission."

Northern cut a slice of fruit, squeezing it into the fizzing liquid, taking his time. "Laura, I am the captain of this ship, the leader. But my authority rests only in my crew's acceptance of me in that position, and my ability to lead. I realize it's in your nature to have a certain contempt for authority. But the plan that we've concocted is the result of much work and I really think we should stick by it."

"But we haven't got the signal! Maybe I can pick it up if I'm closer! I can't wait—another day could mean Cal's death!" What she was trying to pass off as anger was emerging closer to a sob.

"And I understand that. Just as I have my priority, you do as well . . . and in your case it's your brother."

"You can't possibly understand," she said, sprawling in a chair.

"Try me."

"What do you care, Northern?" she asked. "You've got *your* priorities. You've got your precious ship and your delightful crew . . . your home, your family. What do I have? A Federation I've just thumbed my nose at, a blip-ship, and a lost brother, captured by the mean old Jaxdron. You've really got to excuse me, Captain, but as you may recall from your own Federation flunky days, emotional bonds are not exactly encouraged in the Federation scheme of things, and I'm having a bit of a hard time dealing with mine."

Captain Northern sat on his desk and sipped at his drink. "Oh, I remember," he said, looking away. "I also remember something you may be experiencing now."

"Yeah? What's that?" Laura asked suspiciously.

"Guilt."

"Well, I'll grant you I'm guilty as hell of cutting out on the Federation and busting you out of jail," she said, a puzzled expression flitting over her face.

"You feel guilty about your brother."

Laura drew a blank on that. "Huh? I'm risking my neck to get his ass out of a crack."

Captain Northern sighed. "It's perfectly normal, Laura. It comes with the territory. But let me absolve any guilt here. If we are to have a good chance of saving your brother—if indeed he's on Baleful at all—our chances increase exponentially if we work in tandem. The *Starbow* and a blip-ship: surely an unbeatable combination."

"I still say a little scouting expedition on my part wouldn't hurt," she declared, but her indignation rang hollowly in her own ears. "And I don't feel guilty, Captain Tars Pighead Northern, so save your stupid psychology for one of your floozies."

Tars Northern smiled gently. "Laura, it's hard to say what will happen. Although we've got a crack team, we're in unknown territory."

"Yeah. So?"

"Well, I just want to admit that I'm . . . impressed with you. And there is a little girl in you somewhere in that amazing body of yours, and I'm quite charmed by her. But I should add also that I find you, as a woman, quite . . . well, quite beautiful, I suppose."

Laura smiled at that. She rose from her chair and stepped over to him, leaned down, and gave him a soft, wet kiss. Surprised, Northern responded. But Laura pulled her head back and patted him condescendingly on the cheek. "Dream on, bozo," she said, skillfully pulling away from him, mischievous laughter in her eyes.

Northern chuckled as she left, shaking his head as he treated himself to another glass of seltzer, with plenty of lime.

Chapter Twenty-two

CAPTAIN Tars Northern kept the considerable defense capabilities of the starship on optimum alert. For the last four hours before the *Starbow* reached orbital position around the planet known as Baleful, the crew—both human and robot—were posted at battle stations.

So it was rather an anticlimax when there wasn't a sign of any Jaxdron ships before or after they crossed the orbits of Baleful's three moons.

The *Starbow* established a high polar orbit around the world. Captain Northern ordered the sensors turned up full.

Baleful was a Class L planet, only a step away from Terra's Class M, but what a step! Its air was breathable—to its native nomad civilization—but humans needed masks if they were to take it for a long period. Because the Federation could not terraform the world, since this would mean killing the nomads, pressure domes were built. These were mobile and shifted about to avoid the occasional hot spots created by Baleful's parabolic orbit around its binary suns.

After a pass across one of the continents, Captain Northern looked up from Dr. Mish's sensor boards toward where Laura hovered anxiously by communications readouts. "Doesn't look real good, Laura. No sign of activity nonconcurrent with your blip-ship's status-quo info on Baleful. No sign of the military action necessary to assume control, either." Worry ridges appeared on his forehead. "How strange."

"There's got to be some kind of signal!" Laura said emphatically, leaning over Tether Mayz's shoulder. "Northern, you should have let me scout, damn you! We could have missed them by an hour!"

Dr. Mish disagreed. "Sensor sweeps have indicated no spatial disruptions of any kind since our surfacing from Underspace. If the Jaxdrons departed, they did so before we arrived."

"How about any activity within the past five days, Doctor?" Arkm Thur wanted to know. "And how about vectors, if so?"

"I have no desire to chase Jaxdrons farther into enemy territory," Captain Northern stated firmly. "That was not a part of the—"

"That's it!" Laura said, pointing toward an oscillating pattern in the reception unit.

"What's it?" the captain demanded.

"The signal!" she cried. "Mayz, would you turn on the audio for that channel?"

"Yeah. It's Morse code!"

"Morse code?" the communications officer said. "No one uses that anymore. That's as ancient as some of Jitt's jokes!"

"Well, that was our game code when we were kids! Cal found it in some archives and was so fascinated with it, we had to use it!"

Mayz twisted two knobs. Dots and dashes became audible.

"SOS," said Laura, shaking her head and grinning. "How very original, Cal!"

"What's the point of origin, Mayz?"

"Nine degrees north of the equator, Captain." The communications officer, after a moment of analysis, read off the Standard Grid Imposition longitude and latitude.

"Give me a lower orbit, Thur," the captain ordered,

"adjusted toward that signal. Jitt, I want a holo of where that signal is coming from in my tank, as soon as possible."

As the *Starbow* tasted the upper reaches of Baleful's atmosphere, the seas and continents of the planet rolled under its hull majestically, grays and browns and the palest of blues, occasionally blurred by stretches of clouds.

Laura was far too excited to take much notice of the splendor below them.

"You were right, Laura," said Captain Northern. "I haven't the faintest idea how the bugger did it, but he did. Wish we could send him a message back, but I don't think that would be wise."

"Of course he did it, Northern," she said. "Cal is a genius!"

"But how did he know you'd come looking for him?" First Mate Arkm Thur asked.

"Like I told your captain, pal, he knew his sister wouldn't let him down!" She grinned over to Northern. "Talk about moving heaven and earth, eh, Captain?"

"And merely by raising a great deal of hell," Northern murmured, eyes on the vu-tank, where an image was taking translucent shape. It looked like a metallic bubble rising up from the sparsely vegetated ground, agleam in the double suns.

"Can you see anything abnormal on the sensors, Doctor?" Northern asked.

"Standard Federation pressure dome. Model G14, from all signs, with only minimal armament, as a matter of fact," Dr. Mish reported flatly.

"It was my impression, Captain, that this was a Jaxdron-held planet."

"Exactly, Arkm. Everyone's impression, which is perhaps what has kept the Federation away thus far."

"Pardon, sir?"

"Some kind of strange bluff."

"But why?"

"Well, whatever the Jaxdron are up to," Laura said, "I know that my brother Cal is down there, and I intend to hop in my blip-ship and get him." She gave the captain a defiant glance. "Whatever the hell you say."

"You're quite right, Laura," said Captain Northern. "But I'd like to take a shuttle with some armed robots down to back you up."

Laura shrugged. "Whatever you want, Captain, but round 'em up quick, 'cause I'm on my way."

"You'll be on your way, Pilot Shemzak, when we let your ship out of its berth and open the hangars." He got up. "Jitt, estabish synchronous orbit. Arkm, how'd you like to take a little trip?"

"You sure do like to take your chances, don't you, Northern?" Laura said after Arkm had eagerly assented.

"Captain's prerogative, my dear," Northern replied. "Besides, it helps my claustrophobia."

Chapter Twenty-three

SHE felt alive again.

Like a horse straining at its reins, Laura Shemzak, in her XT Mark Nine, yearned for release from the *Starbow*'s bonds. It was almost as though the very fabric of her hull trembled with her impatience.

"C'mon, Northern," she vocalized through her neck-neural connection to the radio band that linked her to the specially souped-up shuttle. "Let's get a move on!"

She'd made her connections with the blip-ship in record time, and her contact with the energies coursing through the intricate mechanism gave her a high like no other she had ever experienced.

"Weapons calibration, dear heart," the voice spoke inside her head. "Give us a minute." For some reason, it annoyed her to have Northern's authoritative sound inside her skull, although constant communication between the two ships was vital in this operation. "You got the hang of your new gizmos?"

"Nothing really new," she returned. "Just improved. I'm surprised that additional biosurgery was needed."

"Well if the Feddies built you and they built the ship, I guess they knew what they were doing."

"They kinda built us all, though, didn't they?" Laura added tersely.

"They certainly would like us to believe that."

Slightly over the time predicted by Captain Northern, the air was removed from the lock, the hangar door opened, and two ships separated from the belly of the *Starbow* like oddly shaped eggs dropping from a metal beast.

For Laura, exhilaration mounted with acceleration; she swooped down through the atmosphere, radiant with sunlight, ablaze with friction. The shuttle was hard pressed to follow on her heels. Planetfall was a rush of splendor, scorching through the air, skirting a sea, playing delicate gyroscope tricks with the air currents above flat desert wastes. She tasted this world, smelled it, inhaled it, sensors wide open and alert for danger.

Within minutes of departure from the low orbit of the *Starbow,* she reached the destination. The pressure dome that emitted the Morse code signal was a brown wart on the desert skin, crusty and hairy with protuberances and antennae. In the seconds it took for Northern and his ponderous shuttle to catch up with her, Laura looped about the structure, energy fields up full, ready to dodge any weapons.

Nothing happened.

She did not scan anything tracking her, although she definitely picked up full-scale electronic activity within the metal and silica shell, indicating life-support systems and intricate computer operations.

"If Cal is in there," Northern's voice sounded in her mind, "he's got plenty to eat and drink and breathe."

"Of course he's in there!" Laura said. "Question is how do *we* get in without exciting any automatic defense systems?"

"How about knocking on the door?"

"Cute, Northern. Real cute."

"Sensors indicate craft entry in the lower northwest quadrant of the dome, Laura. As you might notice from our circling, this thing isn't real great at hovering. We haven't raised anyone on the standard combands. How about if you take a look at one of those doors down there? See if maybe you can throw a switch or something."

"Gotcha, Captain."

Using retros, riding on her antigravs, she descended to the recessed doorway. A quick analysis, a speedy energy futz with the wiring of the identification panel, and the thick doors drew back with a clang.

"No sign of any defensive mechanism inside," she said. "Still, I'm not nuts about doing the cycling procedure."

"Pressure and atmosphere content at this time of the year are only marginally different," reported Arkm Thur. "We can fuse the closing mechanism of the outer door, Laura, and then open the inner door. No one inside will be hurt."

"You got it," Laura said. She found the right metal rod and welded its joint with a laser. Then she drifted into the lock, force field on high.

She triggered no defenses.

"Guess they just don't expect nasty visitors," was her conclusion as she saw to the next door, which only took a nudge to a pair of levers with tractor beams to open.

Reoxygenated air whooshed past Laura, almost refreshingly. She directed her ocular units past the opening and returned her energy flux detection sensors. Nothing amiss . . . just your average Federation pressure dome, efficiently chugging away, more on air-conditioning mode than anything else.

It was like a city in a nutshell, with the interior of the shell painted to look like a pleasant Midwestern America Terran day. She moved forward, entering a different, much smaller world, a microcosmic reflection light-years from its model.

Past the main cluster of buildings lay a large fenced field. Inside were a manor house and a swimming pool and, according to the signal, Cal.

"Come on in, guys, the water's fine," she said, and waited only long enough to see the shuttle nosing in before she sprinted for the field.

"Put her down on this stretch of grass," she said, landing. "I'll leave you plenty of room."

"Roger," said Northern. A moment later he set his

ship down beside the kidney-shaped pool. "Looks deserted. You coming out, Laura, or are you just going to stay in there? The signal's coming from that house, and unless we blast in the roof, we're going to have to go in by foot."

"Have Thur cover us, okay?"

"Sounds reasonable."

She found that her hands trembled slightly as they unlinked her attachments. Her consciousness folded back in to rest behind her eyes, within the sensations of fingers, mouth, ears, body.

Cal, she thought excitedly. I'm going to see Cal again! She realized then that Captain Northern had been right. She did feel guilty—guilty that she had allowed the Federation to take him away from her at all.

Well, no more. When she and Cal were reunited, if the Federation wanted them back, they were going to have to accommodate this brother and sister act! Cal and she would live together again, see each other more, not be so much strangers to each other as in the past years.

She would try to make him see why she'd had to change, she thought as she opened the door and felt the sweet grassy air rush in like a promise. She would show him that even though she could deal with the roughest of spacers, inside she was still his sister, always surprised and delighted with his antics, always understanding and loving.

She checked her sidearm, a power gun in a leather holster. Cal had given it to her last year. "Remember how we used to watch those movie Westerns, Laura?" he had said. "Well, I had this made. Looks like a Colt .45, though it's Federation regulation all the way. You can be like a sheriff, Laura. Wyatt Earp of the spaceways!"

The Federation had not been thrilled with the different design, but they had finally acquiesced to Laura's demands that she carry this, strapped around her waist. The spacers she bunked with would sometimes make fun, until she showed them how fast she could draw it.

When she wore it, it made her realize one of the reasons she cared for Cal so—he had such a sense of play, such imagination!

When Laura stepped down from her ladder onto the grass-matted springy soil, Captain Tars Northern, fully armed with his own more standard power gun and a sensor box, was waiting for her.

"This is the strangest rescue I've ever been involved with," he said, glancing around. "I see no sign of a trap, and no sign of Jaxdron, and yet from all indications you're quite right. Your brother is here. I guess they just didn't expect any kind of rescue mission. And why should they? No one's tried before—no one has been loony enough."

"Shut up and walk, Northern," Laura said. "The signal's coming from that old-style house there."

"I want you to know, Pilot Shemzak," Northern said as they strode toward the gabled mansion a hundred yards away, "that I am not pleased by your insubordinate talk."

"Don't feel bad, Captain," she said. "Everybody gets it. And you know, I keep my word, too. Just as soon as we get Cal out of this place, he'll help you as much as he can . . . on whatever Dr. Mish is working on." She allowed herself a quick scan of the environs. Well kept, pleasant, the place had the very taste of tranquillity. "It doesn't look as though they've been keeping Cal in a dungeon, does it?"

"I still don't like it, Shemzak. No sign of people—or aliens, for that matter."

"Why are you exposing yourself like this, then, Northern? You could have sent Thur out here. For that matter, you could have stayed on the *Starbow*."

Northern shook his head. "Not my speed, Shemzak. I like to participate. Besides, like I say, I owe you. This way I get to pay you back in person."

"Doesn't seem as though it's going to be much of a cost. I . . ." They were now only fifty yards from the arched threshold of the manor house. Past the scrolled columns, Laura could see someone moving. The door opened. A man walked out, waving one arm. She could not make out who it was; he was still in shadow. "Look, Northern!"

"Yes." Northern drew his power gun and pointed it toward the figure.

"What . . .?" Laura said, startled by the motion.

"Just a precaution, Pilot. Can't be too careful, can we?"

The man moved into the full daylight. He wore a simple set of blue trousers and gray shirt and he was smiling. "Laura!" he said. "You found me. It's so good to see you!"

Cal!

He ran toward them, waving happily.

Laura started to run to meet him, then suddenly stopped. It felt as though all of her joints were frozen in place.

"Laura!" Cal called gaily. "Is this a new boyfriend or—"

With practiced speed, Laura Shemzak drew her power gun, aimed it quickly, and shot her brother once directly between the eyes, and then, before he fell, in the heart. Blood spewed as Cal's face contorted into a rictus of surprise and pain. He crumpled onto the ground, shuddering out his last moments of life, face and chest horribly burned from the brief power blasts.

"What the hell!" cried Captain Northern, looking from the body back to Laura.

Horror swept through Laura like ice.

"No!" she wailed. "No!"

Then something struck her in the back of her neck, and someone pulled the plug on reality, leaving less than darkness.

Chapter Twenty-four

AFTER a long day manipulating her holocomp, seeing that the bureaucratic minutiae of the government process were functioning smoothly, Friend Chivon Lasster navigated the halls for home.

Naturally, for security purposes, home was within the labyrinth of Overfriend Headquarters. Sometimes, though she had always been told that the Friends were the most free of the Liberated, she felt as though this honeycomb of rooms and corridors were a prison.

And her crime?

Ambition.

Hands folded under arms as though for warmth, she walked a short distance to the lift to the residential section where she lived, eyes downcast at the dull gray floor.

Her aptitude tests had surprised the system; in every way she was equally adept, mentally and emotionally, in the practical science necessary for starship piloting and the complex needs of the modern administrator. *Perhaps*, she thought morosely, *if they had chosen me to be an administrator, my ambition would have wandered among the stars*. Instead, she had trained as experimental pilot, and her very first assignment had been work with the AI Project, that wondrous fleet of Federation ships that was expected to change the course of interstellar history.

She remembered how, in the course of the work, she had been assigned to help Overfriend Zarpfrin in administration, and how the taste of power that he had shown her changed her.

Yes, imprisoned by ambition, she thought as the lift whisked upward and deposited her on her floor.

But then, she knew very well as a Friend, that ambition was something which was programmed into everyone born under the aegis of the Federated Empire. The system not merely programmed individuals with goals; it also glorified the pain, sentimentalized the anguish of striving for goals, thus creating mental mechanisms that worked and worked and worked for a future that never came, while glorifying an illusory past. This was called "individual attainment for the greater good, with no cost of human freedom."

It worked perfectly.

But no! Friend Chivon Lasster thought. I criticize the very system that gives me meaning, that structures my existence, that works for the causes I believe in.

This system rewards me in the way I deserve to be rewarded, doing the tasks that I should do to serve my society! Uncomfortably, she wondered if she were thinking traitorous thoughts. . . . She felt as tense as a rubber band stretched and stretched. . . .

And how stupid, she thought as she unlocked the door to her apartment. If this state were as totalitarian as my programming notion implies, then there would be a device in my brain now, reading my thoughts. The foundation of the Federation Constitution was liberty for the individual. The methodology had a very important purpose: the survival of the human race!

After all, what if all human-held planets were like the Free Worlds! There could be no united front against the Jaxdron, or any other alien threat, and humanity would soon be under the leash of other species. A small price for the greater freedom of the individual as reflected in the macrocosm of their state!

No, she thought, flicking on a light. Zarpfrin and the Overfriends were quite right. The ontological disaster that was nationalism must be opposed at the root; look how it had scarred the twenty-first and twenty-second centuries. Humans must look to a higher plane, and that plane was the confederation . . . the system that had molded her. It must not be questioned, must not be undermined—certainly not by one of its primary officers!

She slipped into a comfortable robe, allowed herself the luxury of a narcotic water pipe, and slipped a tape of a popular drama serial she enjoyed into the cube tube.

When the segment had run its course, she still felt anxiety. She had not used Andrew for a while.

Soon the spectral, fatherly figure of her Companion sat before her.

She told him about Kat Mizel, and how through her Tars Northern might be brought back to Terra to face trial. "I would like to see him brought to justice," she concluded. "I should like to see him punished as an example to the people of the Federation of what happens to a traitor," she said tersely.

Ghostly hands clasped together thoughtfully under Andrew's nose; he was a brilliantly programmed simulacrum of human behavior. "This is not the song you were singing before, Chivon Lasster."

"Perhaps my talks with you have been therapeutic. Perhaps these pathological thoughts bordering on the obsessive are clearing up."

"And yet you are clearly upset at the story that Kat Mizel has told. . . . And her relationship with Northern troubles you."

"I have no reason to feel wronged in this instance, although the state was damaged by Northern's betrayal. It is well that the illusory bond he constructed to fool me was disrupted. It had confused my higher moral and ethical values."

"You called me up to tell me that?"

"You're supposed to help me, dammit," Lasster said, fury blossoming in her eyes. "You're supposed to listen! Just listen! I . . . I just want to tell you that I am better now. I have some travel ahead of me to help oversee this operation. Zarpfrin has already left. I won't be calling you up for a while. . . ." She looked at him, and chuckled to herself. "Wait a moment. What am I saying this for? You're just a construct! You don't really exist, not as a human being does. I'm treating you as if you really care what happens to me. You're just a machine."

The classically handsome face of the Companion looked at her with an interested expression. "And what, Friend Lasster, are you?"

"I'm not in the mood for any sophistry. What are you talking about?"

"I mean, what makes you so sure that you know who and what I am? We've not discussed this before, Chivon."

"You're . . . well, you're just a fantastically complex program running through a matrix of biochips."

"As complex as your program. As interconnected as your matrix of neurons."

"What are you trying to say, Andrew?"

He smiled. "I am saying, Chivon Lasster, that there are things you don't know. About many things. About me."

"I don't understand."

"Perhaps it is time to explain," said Andrew. "At least about me."

"No! No, this must be some kind of new therapy and I'm just too tired. I need to go to bed, I have a busy day tomorrow, and well, good-bye, Andrew."

She turned the computer off, and Andrew instantly disappeared.

She was tired. She knew she could sleep now. She took off her robe, and slipped under the covers of her bed. Sleep was not far away.

Some time later, she awoke, startled.

Something had touched her.

She pushed herself up.

He was even easier to see in the darkness, constructed of a kind of gentle phosphorescence, sculpted from light.

"Chivon," he said somberly. "We really must talk."

Chapter Twenty-five

SHE awoke suddenly, gasping, from the most dreadful nightmare of her life.

Cal, she thought. Cal! Eyes wild, she looked up. Northern's presence registered. "Let me go," she said. "What happened?"

Her head hurt terribly.

"I had to knock you out, Laura," Northern said. "Something is wrong with you. Very wrong."

Desperately she looked toward the manor house.

Cal lay sprawled on the lawn, legs and arms akimbo, eyes glazed over, face sheeted with blood.

"I . . . did . . . that . . ." she said, numbness spreading over her as her inner world shattered. "What . . . why?" She found herself clutching Northern as though for dear life. She sobbed, feeling as though she must be losing her mind.

"They wanted him dead, can't you see? I should have known, I should have realized," Northern said. "They must have put a motor override implant in you, primed for the first sight of your brother, the first sound of his voice."

A figure moved beside them. "Will she be okay?"

Laura looked up.

Standing over them was Cal.

She reached for her sidearm, unable to control herself.

Her hand grasped empty air. She shuddered and spasmed. Cal moved away.

"Get back into the house for now," Northern ordered. "And tell the other one to stay put. The implant is tearing her apart."

The wave passed, leaving her drained and limp.

"Listen to me carefully, Laura," Northern said, strongly and steadily. "You did not kill the real Cal Shemzak. Nor was that the real Cal Shemzak."

Relief and hope filled her.

"I don't understand," she whispered, transfixed between the desire to believe and the reality she had experienced.

Northern gripped her firmly, supportively. "Come over here, Laura," he said, pulling her up. He led her to the prostrate body of the dead Cal Shemzak. "Take a look."

Laura forced herself to gaze down upon the havoc her gun had wreaked upon the body. Through the ugly red of the wounds, metal glinted, wires ran. "A cyborg copy," she whispered. "A simulacrum."

"When you pulled that gun, Laura, and gave this thing two of the best, I thought Dr. Mish and I had misread you somehow, that we had some monster in our midst. But the look of horror in your eyes saved you. They set you up, Laura, don't you see? Zarpfrin has gotten even more devious. No wonder they wanted you to find your brother. They knew you didn't have a prayer of coming back—but they also knew you had a damned good chance of finding your brother. And when you found him, they wanted you to kill him."

"Why?" Laura whispered.

"Easy. They don't want the Jaxdron to have him. They prefer him dead."

"My operation . . . the different biomech. Of course," Laura said. "I was . . . set up."

"They knew you'd go off half-cocked, Laura. Off on your valiant quest for your brother, not even thinking why they would allow such a thing, why they gave you their new blip-ship. And while they were fitting you for it, they stuck a simple override chip in your optical nerve leading straight to your trigger finger. Mish probably interpreted it as part of your blip-ship circuitry. One sight of Cal Shemzak. Zap. All problems over. And they knew that you'd be so devastated by the action that if you didn't immediately kill yourself, you'd be open to Jaxdron attack. And I dare say, on the off chance neither of those possibilities were to occur, they've got an alert out to blast your blip-ship upon sight."

Laura despaired. She leaned her head against Northern's shoulder, so filled with emptiness she could not be angry, could not even cry.

"A pawn," she said. "All along, I thought I was such hot stuff, and I'm a pawn."

He rubbed her shoulder comfortingly. "Yes, and so was I, Laura, until I opted out. . . ."

She broke away from him, fighting hard for self-control. "And I'll not be your pawn either, Northern, so get your paws off me!"

Northern reacted as though he'd been slapped. A flash of vulnerability, of hurt, appeared in usually dark, unreadable eyes, then was gone.

Laura looked down at the body and said, contemptuously, "Why the hell did the Jaxdron make a copy of Cal?" She looked up at the front of the manor. "Two copies, I mean."

"Three, actually," Northern said. "There's another one in there. I don't know why, Laura. The others tell me that the Jaxdron left just yesterday, taking Cal with them. They claim they might be able to tell us where they went, for all the good that will do. Understandably, they're rather confused themselves. We've scanned them for any kind of problem: they read clean. Laura, I'm going to bring them back on the *Starbow* for Dr. Mish to analyze. There's even more to all this than I thought, and I have to accept my involvement, and the *Starbow*'s involvement."

"And what, pray tell, is going to stop me from murdering them on sight?" Laura said in a bitter, harsh voice.

"Dr. Mish has the knowledge, the equipment," Northern said softly. "If you'll trust us . . . if you'll allow him, he'll perform the operation necessary to remove the implant that must be in your head."

"And why should I trust anybody?" Laura said. "The whole universe is laughing behind my back now."

"Well, Laura, if that's true, then the only thing to do is to laugh with it."

She spun on him, anger flaring. "And what's that goddamn supposed to mean, Northern? I mean, I just took a shot at the only person who means a hill of beans to me, and you expect me to laugh? I take a blow like this to my sense of self-confidence, and you're expecting a giggle? I mean, if this can happen, who can say if any of my actions are really my own? Maybe all I am is a bunch of implants responding, triggering. Right, you jerk. My whole universe is crumbling, and you want me to laugh?"

"That's not what I said, Pilot Shemzak, and we haven't got time to argue. First Mate Thur reports no other sign of life in this pressure dome. I want to get back to the *Starbow*. Now, if you'll get back into your blip-ship and close those beautiful eyes of yours, I'll hustle the Shemzak twins on board the shuttle and we'll get out of this place."

Laura trudged back to her ship, climbed the ladder, and went through connection procedure. Everything in her struggled to maintain her composure, her equilibrium. She feared that if she allowed one bit of self-control go, she would simply lose her mind.

As she merged bioelectrically, neuronically, spiritually with her blip-ship, even her usual sense of transcendence eluded her.

Cal was still alive, though no thanks to her. And if Northern was right, if Dr. Mish could cut out her accursed Federation implant, then she'd be free of that wretched bunch forever, free to find Cal, to start some kind of new life . . . although God alone knew what that life would be.

"Eeny, meeny, miny, mo," she said once her communicator was warmed up. Her head still hurt from Northern's blow. "Can I start up my visuals?"

"Affirmative, Laura," came Northern's voice immediately. "We've got your brother's copies on board the shuttle, out of sight."

"Wonderful. This blip-ship's got a little more weapons power than my revolver. Speaking of which, where is the thing?"

"Safely tucked away in here, safety on, Laura. Now if you'll—"

A sudden message from the *Starbow* interrupted them.

"You'd better get back here, Captain," Dansen Jitt's shaky voice said. "We've got trouble."

Chapter Twenty-six

DANSEN Jitt hated space battles.

He despised the sounds of lasers raking across hulls, dreaded the pyrotechnics sizzling in the blackness of space, disliked even the smell of burned circuitry from the overloads that invariably resulted from such uncivilized space brawls.

Most of all, though, Jitt hated the idea of dying.

So, when the two starships dropped out of nowhere and began firing salvos at the *Starbow*, Jitt, manning the conn, was less than pleased.

Fortunately, he had been cautious; the dazzling blasts from the bizarrely shaped vessels were easily deflected by the primary force screen of the *Starbow*, amplified two steps above normal.

Nonetheless, the bridge shook, and Jitt was hard pressed to maintain his cool. First, he ordered evasive maneuvers; second, he ordered Comm Officer Mayz to establish contact with Captain Northern on the surface of Baleful; third, he called crew members to their defensive posts with the emergency klaxon.

Then, with the Jaxdron ships diving in formation for another attack on the *Starbow*, Dansen Jitt took the spare few seconds to panic.

Fortunately, everyone else was too busy to notice him

grow pale as milk, no one saw him shake desperately, no one noticed him closing his eyes, straining with all his might not to throw up.

"I warned you, Northern!" he cried silently, and some of his fear bled off into anger. "If we all die, it's your fault."

When he opened his eyes again, he first saw vu-screens. Both Jaxdron whip-ships were slightly smaller and thinner than the *Starbow*. They moved fast. Sleek needles stitching through the night they came, power rays stretched out before them like deadly headlights.

"Don't they want to talk this over?" Jitt whined. "Mayz, see if you can raise them on the radio. Maybe they've got the wrong ship. . . . Yeah, assure them we're not Federation—"

The whole ship shook with new blasts against the force shields. Jitt fell back into his chair.

The *Starbow* answered with a volley of its own that struck one of the retreating ships, but to no apparent effect.

"We felt that on the secondary field, Lieutenant," Gemma Naquist said. "Shall I set up a tertiary?"

"Yes!" Jitt said.

"Lieutenant," said Officer Mayz. "No response to our signal. But I am getting an interesting reading—"

Suddenly Dr. Mish appeared at the door. He stalked forward, frowning, and motioned Silver Zenyo away from the sensor boards.

"How peculiar," he said, gazing down at the read-outs.

"What's wrong, Doctor, besides the fact that we're in a bunch of trouble?" Jitt said, shakily.

"Those ships have got an extremely advanced form of analysis beam focused on us. Their aggressive activity seems to be masking the fact that they're simply seeing what we're made of." He shook his head and smiled wryly. "Not good enough, fellows. Nice try."

"What are you talking about, Doctor?" Jitt said.

"Lieutenant, I'm reading a great deal of power inside those ships," the doctor said somberly. "And if they wanted to use that power—"

"Here they come again!" Silver Zenyo shrieked quite unprofessionally.

The white power beams streaking out before the whip-ships suddenly changed to bright blue. They sparked against the periphery of the force screen with a dazzling display of spectrum distortion as power beams from the *Starbow*'s port side slashed forward to meet the attacker.

Silver Zenyo gasped, painted nails reaching into her hair, teeth clenched, eyes open with pain.

"Jitt!" Communications Officer Mayz shouted. "The strangest signals . . ."

The hull rivets and structural joints of the *Starbow* seemed to shriek with outrage at the pressure exerted upon them by the enemy power beams.

The crew members on the bridge shook like marionettes shorn of strings.

"Nothing for it," said Dr. Mish, staggering toward a control board. "I'm going to have to cut in the extradimensional reserve!"

"What in God's name is that?" Dansen Jitt cried. But Dr. Mish seemed too busy to answer—nor did he seem to do much at the control board, simply grabbing hold of two bus bars, then becoming statue-stiff.

Within moments the vibrations stopped. Dansen Jitt steadied himself by leaning against the command chair. A sudden change in the vu-screen attracted his attention. Purplish red beams of astonishing width seemed to emanate from each pod on the *Starbow*'s radii. These converged upon the two Jaxdron ships, holding them motionless.

"Some sort of tractor beam," said Mayz. "But I've never seen anything like it."

"Quickly!" Jitt ordered. "Blast them!"

The weapons officers aimed the beamers, but did not fire.

"What's wrong?" Jitt demanded.

"All the power is apparently being sapped by those beams, sir!" came the answer.

Jitt turned to Dr. Mish, who maintained the same

position, eyes closed in intense concentration. He did not respond at all to Jitt when the little man called his name.

Jitt turned his attention back to the vu-screen. The Jaxdron whip-ships were struggling to escape the tractor beams and not succeeding.

"What can we do, sir?" asked one of the crew.

"Apparently Mish is counting on Laura Shemzak and Captain Northern to disable or destroy those ships," said Jitt. "He's throwing everything we've got into keeping them there."

"Lieutenant Jitt," said Silver Zenyo. "Sensor readings show a tremendous power surge of some kind on one of the Jaxdron ships."

"Look!" Mayz pointed to the primary vu-screen. "Something has broken away from one of those ships. It's gotten free of the tractor beams!"

"Some kind of boarding boat!" Jitt said. He struck one of the controls on his chair. "Red alert! Red alert!" he cried breathlessly. "Break out in-ship weapons and prepare for alien boarding!"

Chapter Twenty-seven

WHEN the blip-ship and its attendant shuttle rose from the globe that was Baleful, they were immediately confronted by the sight of the Jaxdron whip-ships caught in the *Starbow*'s tractor beams.

"I'm going to take out their engines if I can," radioed Laura Shemzak. "You get back to the ship, Captain, and stow those false brothers away somewhere so that I don't shoot them on sight!"

"Roger, Laura," replied Captain Northern. "Good luck—wait a moment. We're getting something from the *Starbow*."

Laura tuned in to the *Starbow*'s frequency and immediately received Jitt's voice. "Mayday! Mayday! Captain, a small Jaxdron ship has pierced our defensive shields and is docking right now, drilling a hole through Alpha airlock, closest to the bridge." A terrible din was audible through the speakers—then a loud explosion. "Captain, they're through. They've boarded!"

"Damn!" Captain Northern said. "Pilot Shemzak, reroute and destroy Jaxdron sucker-ship attached to *Starbow*. Then resume previous plans."

"Yes, sir," said Laura, not questioning the orders at all. "Over and out." She banked away from formation with Northern's shuttlecraft and accelerated toward the *Starbow*'s position.

The sight of the surging energies locking the ships together was quite spectacular, but she didn't pause to admire the view, streaking in as fast as possible toward the indicated airlock. Sure enough, there was a small ship of a strange trapezoid design attached to the hull of the *Starbow*.

Laura's excellent sensors showed no shields whatsoever around the invading craft. Good. She wouldn't have to waste energy.

Her first salvo caught the vessel square in the rear, ripping it in half with a violent explosion. Torn fragments scattered every which way, some taking up an orbit around the *Starbow*. A brief release of gases shot from the opening—and then the *Starbow* automatically sealed itself tight again.

"I got it, folks," she said. "Now I'm going to see what I can do about the big guys,"

She righted her blip-ship and accelerated toward the two Jaxdron ships, careful to stay out of range of the peculiar and powerful tractor beams that held them rigid.

Three aliens emerged from the blown-open airlock—but they were not Jaxdron. They were robots—squat, human-shaped—who carried streamlined energy rifles and immediately headed straight for the bridge.

A contingent of Dr. Mish's robots, armed themselves and led by General Patton, guarded the entrance to the bridge and met the invading robots' fire with fire of their own, delaying them long enough for another party of Mish's robots, led by Napoleon Bonaparte, to attack them from the back.

It was at this point that Laura's successful attack upon the invading ship blew the entire conflict into complete chaos. The rearmost alien robot and one of the defending robots were destroyed in the explosion—and the other two alien robots were blown directly into Patton's party, creating a strange metallic free-for-all of battling fists and fire.

Jitt monitored all this with growing apprehension.

"They're getting closer!" he said, holding his energy pistol nervously.

"They've broken through," he went on, staring in horror at the screen. The bronze and black pair of robots, previously a berserker blur, exploded through the mass of warring simulacrums in a blast of light. While one of the robots kept the defenders at bay, the other worked with his energy gun at the door leading to the bridge.

"Oh, God," said Jitt "it's not built to stand that kind of punishment!"

The robot facing Mish's creations took a blast full in the neck; its head toppled off. Its weapon dropped from its hands, but it blindly kept its stand, shielding its fellow from the blasts of the simulacra.

With a deafening noise, the door mechanism snapped. The alien robot tore the metal as it wrenched the door open. Close up, Jitt could see three black-lensed oculars swiveling as though searching for something. A beam hit its torso to little effect. Jitt recovered enough from his terror to fire off a blast. But the robot ignored both, focusing its oculars upon the figure of Dr. Michael Mish, still frozen over his set of controls.

"Doctor!" cried Silver Zenyo. "Watch out!"

But the doctor did not move, and the power beam caught him full in the back, blowing him away from the board, crumpling him into a smoking heap in a corner.

"Doctor!" Dansen Jitt yelled. He leaped toward his fallen comrade, putting a chair between himself and the alien robot as it exploded, sparks flying from its head and torso. What was left of the big machine crashed to the floor, twitched, and was still.

The only sound was the whir of intake fans straining to deal with all the smoke.

"It was after the doctor," Dansen Jitt said. "But why?"

"Lieutenant," said Silver Zenyo, her uniform torn,

her hair mussed, her makeup smeared. She lifted a cracked fingernail and pointed at the vu-screen. "I think your answer's there!"

Jitt looked—and something touched his mind, a whisper-vision, a voice, a broadcast of incredible depth and power.

And Dansen Jitt knew the real meaning of fear.

Laura Shemzak had been involved with a number of space melees during her career, with a solid background of countless hours in training simulation, with sub-liminal attitude adjustment that made her view the interchange of lasers and photon torpedoes and what all as rather a sport. She could dance around a bigger ship like a bee about a bush, using the generally superior biotechnology and weaponry of her blip-ship to the utmost advantage over much larger and higher-powered vessels. Her ultrahuman intuitive capabilities allowed her to anticipate and dodge power beams her force fields were incapable of dealing with.

However, when she hovered within five hundred meters of the ships hung in the tractor beams like flies in sparkling amber, her sensors immediately noted that none of the weapons blisters seemed prepared to fire upon her. So she scooted about the periphery of the tractor beams' influence, trying to determine the best way to put one of the ships' engines out of commission.

Up close, she could see why they were called whip-ships. They were long and cylindrical, with nodes and blisters and ports in oddly symmetrical patterns, and a strange elasticity. Portions of the hulls were translucent, revealing odd and definitely alien inner workings; she could not make head or tail of her sensor sweep data.

I wonder if Cal is somewhere in one of those ships, she thought to herself, trying to pick up any kind of readings with identifiable patterns.

No, she concluded. There was nothing human in either of those ships, unless the Jaxdron had shielded Cal somehow.

Finally she gave up and just decided to let one of the

ships have a strong taste of her firepower to the rear.

She fired.

The blast made the stern of the whip-ship glow red briefly, but nothing more.

Damn! What kind of stuff was this hull made of, anyway?

She had no chance to find out, for just as she fired again, the tractor beams disappeared, and the Jaxdron ships streaked away, causing her shot to miss entirely and leaving her uncharacteristically surprised.

Her intuition, however, was strong enough to use a starboard impeller to abandon her present position, which prevented her from being more than stunned by a blast of tremendous proportions from one of the ships.

And there was more. . . . Subliminally she detected some kind of psychic broadcast, content unrecognizable.

She spun away through space away from the *Starbow*, struggling for control. By the time she was able to right herself, the Jaxdron ships were too far away for her to have any hope of pursuing them further.

What the hell had happened? That boarding vessel . . . The creatures inside must have gotten to the controls. A kind of panic hit her, a fear, a pain. . . .

She realized that she didn't want these people to be hurt. For some reason she had a feeling for them, a concern. . . .

Quickly she sped to the boarding dock.

Chapter Twenty-eight

LAURA docked within the *Starbow* and made it to the bridge in record time.

Smoke still hung in the air over the wreckage of the robots, both human simulacrum and alien, that lay strewn all over. Arkm Thur and Captain Northern were busy assaying the damage.

Dansen Jitt, in the command chair, looked as though he had just taken poison and was waiting for it to take effect.

In the corner lay Dr. Mish, twisted circuitry hanging from his blackened chest.

"Dr. Mish!" Laura cried, stepping back with horror. She blinked.

"Dr. Mish is a robot?" she said.

Captain Northern walked over to the still form and twisted off the head. "Alas, poor Yorick," he said.

The eyes in the separated head seemed to light. "Watch out for that poisoned sword tip, my friend." The voice emerged from the mouth cavity, though the jaws did not move.

Northern related to Laura what had happened. "Somehow," he finished, "the Jaxdron knew that to cut that tractor beam, they had to break Mish's concentration. So they sent their boarding robots and accomplished that task quite handily."

"Alas," said a powerful voice, seeming to throb through the air with the authority of God himself. "I was locked into my interface with that particular construct, and its destruction did indeed . . . ah . . . break my concentration."

"And?"

"Amazing, Captain," said the voice. "Quite like nothing I've ever encountered before. And during their little strafing run they hit me with a remarkably powerful analysis ray."

"Oh?"

"Fortunately, it wasn't powerful enough for them to get a full reading."

Laura shook her head. "This is too much for me, guys. I shoot my own brother, who turns out not to be my brother at all but one of a trio of clone-cyborgs. A couple of Jaxdron ships thumb their noses at us. I come back to find Dr. Mish lying in pieces on the floor, and talking to us like Zeus from Mount Olympus."

"There are more things in heaven and earth, Laura Shemzak, than are dreamt of in your philosophy," replied Northern softly.

"Captain," said Dansen Jitt, with haunted eyes. "I know which way they're going. I know where they have taken Cal Shemzak. Somehow my mind touched something inside those ships."

"Very good, Jitt," said Northern. "I knew you'd be worth your keep one day. Set a course toward wherever that place is, immediately."

"Captain, I realize that this is familiar, but I saw that something terrible, something worse than even imagination can describe, will happen if we follow those ships. I can't explain it, but please believe me—"

"The wolf or its pack, Jitt?"

"The pack, Captain, with a few werewolves thrown in for good measure."

"Set the course, Jitt. I'll examine your report at my leisure. And I want a full analysis of these Jaxdron robots." He looked down at Mish's head, then tossed it back on the floor. "Crew meeting in an hour. There are some things that I must explain to you all now that this has happened. Also, there are items to discuss with you, Pilot Shemzak. I think you deserve some explanations." He turned to the clearly upset crew members. "You all deserve explanations."

Laura took time for a quick shower, so when she entered the stateroom for the meeting, she felt, although baffled, at least refreshed.

The lights were turned low, and small bulbs here and there created a distinct candlelight effect.

Captain Northern and his crew sat in silence around the table, solemn and sober. They all wore military outfits of unique design, rich with crests, aiguillettes, trim, ties, standing collars, and epaulets. The silver, maroon, and gray seemed to glow softly.

"Please take the empty chair, Pilot Shemzak," Captain Northern instructed.

"What is this, church?" Laura said, sitting down, impressed with the aura of ceremony.

"Not quite, Pilot Shemzak," the captain responded softly.

"I rather like that notion," the reverberating, timbreful voice said.

Laura started. "Well, I figured it out, Dr. Mish, or whatever you are. You're really the ship's computer, aren't you, operating that robot by remote control! Am I right, Northern?"

"Partially, Laura. However, the rather annoying voice you hear belongs not just to the ship's computer. It is, quite simply, the voice of the *Starbow*. You sit in a sentient ship, Pilot Shemzak."

"AI Project," Laura murmured. "Of course!" she said loudly. "Artificial Intelligence. So you stole an artificially intelligent ship from the Federation, Northern?"

"Please," said the voice of the *Starbow*. "I dislike the term 'artificial.' I am less artificial than you, Pilot Shemzak, and quite a bit more intelligent."

"Whatever. That answers some questions. I always wondered why they didn't have AI stuff in the Federation. Looks as though they gave it a try and didn't like the results. Am I right?"

"Something like that, Laura," Captain Northern said. "There were five ships like the *Starbow*. Overfriend Zarpfrin was in charge of the operation. As soon as the artificially intelligent ships were able to think for themselves, they decided they did not care to work on the assignments that the Federation had in store for them. They planned to depart Federation space, but there was a traitor among the pilots of the AI project. I don't know who it was. Suffice it to say, the *Starbow* and I were the only ship and pilot to escape Federation control."

"I can see why you haven't any particular fondness for the Feddies or the Friends," said Laura.

"No love lost, Laura," said Northern.

"And so you turned pirate."

"Necessary to survive, dear lady. But there's more than that to our little group. And we haven't let you have any idea until now because we were not sure of your loyalties. I take it, with the events of late, that we may now consider you a free agent?"

"You sure can. I've got a blip-ship, and I've got some keen hatred in my heart. There's no room for a loyalty to a system I've long despised."

"I think we can trust you," said Captain Northern. "What do you say, Doctor?"

"I would say, Captain, that she is as good a bet as any of the lot we've picked up so far."

"Excellent. And how say the rest of you?"

The other crew members agreed that Laura was reasonably trustworthy, in light of the situation.

"Very well, then," said Northern gravely but with a trace of a twinkle in his eye. "Pilot Laura Shemzak, as captain of the *Starbow* I should like to invite you to renounce your affiliation with the Federated Empire of Terran Planets and join our crew in loyalty and service. Your word will be your bond."

"I—" Laura began.

Northern held up his hand, preempting her. "Oh yes. One more little thing you should know before you make any promises. Gemma, I think it would be appropriate for you to have a word here."

Gemma Naquist stood. "I believe what the captain wishes me to disclose, Laura, is the fact that although we serve no one, the crew of the *Starbow*, though certainly a motley bunch with amazingly disparate philosophies, hold a common ideal."

"Down with the Federation?"

"Not quite, Laura. In principle, we've nothing against the ideal of a linking form of government between planets. We should like to see some sort of network established between the Free Worlds for mutual support and protection. We should like to see the current form of government in the Federation dissolved. You might say that, in addition to being pirates and mercenaries, we are also revolutionaries. In joining us, you would become an outcast. There are Free Worlds that welcome us, but also Free Worlds that do not, and sometimes it is difficult to tell the difference."

"What Gemma means," Northern said, "is that this is not exactly a stable way of life."

"By no means," continued Naquist. "And by allying yourself with us, you burn your bridges."

"I'm not exactly a political kind of person," Laura said. "But since I'm definitely revolting against the Federation, I guess I don't mind being labeled a revolutionary. It certainly sounds nobler than 'pirate.' "

"I take it, then, Laura Shemzak, that you agree to become one of our number and that we have your oath of loyalty to the *Starbow*," Captain Northern said.

"Just as long as you help me find my brother," Laura answered. "My real brother."

"As you may have gleaned from our attitudes, that serves us well enough."

Laura chuckled humorlessly. "Yeah, if we can get ahold of Cal, I'm sure he's not going to care to help the Federation any longer."

"You will swear allegiance, then?"

"You know, I've never done that sort of thing before," Laura said. "With the Federation, it's all knee-jerk. You serve it because you are programmed to serve it. The only promises I've ever made were to Cal."

Captain Northern said, "With your promises you define yourself."

Laura thought for a second. She looked around at the assembled crew, and a strange wave of emotion swept over her, along with a realization: they wanted her among them. She could belong to something bigger than herself that didn't want to crush her, mold her, shape her toward its own ends.

She was strangely moved.

"Yes," she said softly. "I'll join you."

Captain Northern nodded and smiled softly. "You are very welcome among us, Pilot Laura Shemzak." His eyes caught hers in a disarming way, a personal message that seemed more than just a welcome.

Vulnerable to this new emotion, she found herself becoming lost in that gaze, intrigued by the mystery those eyes held.

She caught herself.

"Well then, Dr. *Starbow* or Mish or whatever the hell you're calling yourself, if you're just disassembled pieces now, how are you going to get this damned implant out of my head?" She tapped her temple as she gazed up toward the ceiling. "I want to talk to those Cal clones, not shoot them."

The voice answered.

"For temporary purposes, while I construct a robot body to suit my fancy, I can control one of my other robots, and thus perform the necessary operation. As a matter of fact—"

The door opened and a uniformed robot stepped in and began speaking in the *Starbow*'s voice.

"—my Genghis Khan model is quite dexterous in such work."

Pilot Laura Shemzak shook her head and sighed.

Chapter Twenty-nine

"CAPTAIN," Dansen Jitt said, "I'm sorry to bother you, but I really must speak with you."

The voice filtered through the intercom of the captain's cabin.

Northern, freed for a while from the *Starbow*'s continual surveillance of his drinking, had poured himself a hefty tumbler of brandy and was lying pleasantly semi-comatose upon his bunk. He roused himself and let the slight man in.

"Yes, Jitt?" he said blearily, only half noticing the man's frazzled, gaunt look.

"It's about what happened on the bridge, sir. About the psychic broadcast from the Jaxdron."

"You set the course, didn't you?"

For whatever reason, the Jaxdron had notified the *Starbow* of the next stage of their quest: a planet called Snar'shill, clear to the other side of the Fault, on the fringe of the spiral arm holding Terra and most of the Human-inhabited worlds.

"Yes, but Captain, why should they give us their destination unless it's some sort of trap?" Jitt said nervously.

"Most likely it is, Jitt. So what? We took that chance

on this little jaunt, and we're just going to have to take that chance again."

"There's more, Captain. What I saw . . . You know I've a small amount of psi ability."

"Jitt, can't I read this on your report?"

Jitt brushed past him and poured himself a drink, something that the man seldom did. He downed it with an unsteady hand.

"Northern, I'm not a strong talent at all; maybe the odd flash, you know, and an intuitive grasp of mathematics, odds, and navigation. My premonitions have always been weak little squiggles in my head, which I . . . tend to amplify.

"But, Captain, up there on that bridge . . . that surge of thought . . . that vision I got. That was strong stuff."

"Okay, Dansen," the captain said softly and respectfully. "I'll bite. Shoot."

"It wasn't anything literal or linear. A succession of images, a mélange of emotions, a feeling of . . . I don't know, Captain—the unknown." Jitt stared off into empty space. "I experienced alien life I never imagined existed. Whole cycles of life and death in just a breath. I saw suns being born and suns dying. And then I saw the planet, and I recognized it. Snar'shill, in the Dominus cluster. And I heard a voice saying, 'This is where we'll be.' And the tone was taunting, as though it were saying, 'Follow us if you dare.' "

"Yes, that is the direction they seem to be headed."

"But Captain, there was more. I saw . . . felt . . . blood . . . and destruction . . . upheaval. I saw fleets battling. Thousands of ships, Captain, locked in deadly battle, in atmosphere, on seas, on land, and in space. And it was a conflict that went on forever, Captain. An eternal battle."

"Go on, Jitt."

"Captain, I'm not sure I should."

"Please."

"Very well. Three images that troubled me the most. I saw Pilot Laura Shemzak, smiling. I saw you lying on the ground, quite dead. And I saw the explosive destruction of the *Starbow*. And the weird voice that was the voice of the Jaxdron seemed to whisper to me, 'Yes, come, follow, and experience all this fun, all these games.' "

"That's quite a plateful, Dansen," said the captain.

"Captain, I urge you to reconsider our involvement in this affair. Believe me, the portents are not good."

"We can release you from your enlistment here, Dansen. There must be some world, somewhere, that will have you."

Dansen Jitt sighed. "You know that I can't—no, *won't* do that. This is my . . . family, my home. Whatever its destiny, that is a destiny I must share."

Captain Northern placed his hand on the navigator's shoulder. "That is good to know, Dansen. You are like a brother to me."

"Then you're going to stay on course? You intend to follow the Jaxdron and Cal Shemzak?"

Captain Northern nodded. "This is more than trying to reunite a feisty, bad-tempered young woman and her snot-nosed brother. This involves more, even, than the safety and alliance of the Free Worlds." He looked into his glass and swirled the last of the brandy. "We're dealing, Dansen, with a threat to the very fabric of reality that we call our universe."

Northern clinked his glass against Dansen Jitt's and then gulped down its contents.

Epilogue

ON the planet Nocturnus, the darkness itself seemed to wail with the voice of winds.

The man's personal starship—a sleek and expensive model that shone more like the jewels of royalty than anything utilitarian—had landed by the settlement as though on wings of flame. He descended on the extended ramp to the icy ground, flanked by a pair of robot bodyguards. A group of creatures awaited him with a reverent silence due to a celestial messenger.

Humanoid, his welcoming committee all wore furs with hoods that concealed their features. The man wore a thermal suit, and was quite comfortable despite the chill of the swirling winds that cut through the mountainous landscape. Past the icy field where the starship had landed lay a scatter of Quonset huts.

"You are expected," a gravelly-voiced alien said in standard Galactic. "Please accompany us."

The man agreed and followed the silent party. Their boots crunched through the snow. The robots to either side were alert, sensors wide open for possible danger.

At the edge of the settlement, where the snow gave way to warm, wet pavement, one of the aliens turned.

"Please leave all weapons at this checkpoint."

Lamps revealed hints of a cluster of eyes, a round protruding mouth.

The robots gripped the handles of their pistols, ready to use them.

"It's all right," said the man. "Obey the request."

The robots handed over the weapons.

"This way."

The man and the robots followed the aliens to a central hut, larger than the rest.

The door cycled open.

Warmth gushed out. The interior was dimly lit. A fishy, oily smell was immediately discernible.

The man took a deep breath. This was the crucial step. Upon this meeting rested the fate of years of planning.

He stepped into the room, which seemed swathed in rich, light-spattered cloth, a section of starry night sky scissored from the firmament.

A figure separated itself from the darkness at the far end, a thing clearly not at all humanoid.

"I am here," said the man.

The creature spoke a guttural gurgling language, which was translated by a mechanism dangling from the ceiling.

"Greetings, Overfriend Zarpfrin," said the Jaxdron Master General. "Please rest yourself. We have much to speak about."

Zarpfrin smiled and nodded. "Yes, we do."

MORE SCIENCE FICTION ADVENTURE!